WELCOME TO THE BSC, ABBY

**Other books by
Ann M. Martin**

WELCOME TO THE BSC, ABBY

Ann M. Martin

AN
APPLE
PAPERBACK

SCHOLASTIC INC.
New York Toronto London Auckland Sydney

Cover art by Hodges Soileau

ISBN 0-590-22874-9

12 11 10 9 8 7 6 5 4 3 2 1   5 6 7 8 9/9 0/0

Printed in the U.S.A.   40

First Scholastic printing, October 1995

For Sara Ruth Bell

The author gratefully acknowledges
Nola Thacker
for her help in
preparing this manuscript.

WELCOME TO THE BSC, ABBY

CHAPTER 1

The people in Stoneybrook name their cars. Or at least, some of them do. Such as a neighbor of mine. Residing in her driveway are two cars with names — the Junk Bucket and the Pink Clinker.

I do not need to describe these cars. The names tell their stories. In fact, that they even *have* names tells a story in itself.

But when in Rome do as the Romans do. And when in Stoneybrook, do as the Stoneybrookians do, right?

"I dub this . . . this . . . means of transportation the Wheeze Wagon," I said as the Stoneybrook Middle School bus wheezed, heaved, coughed, and groaned to a stop. It gave a final lurch just as I stood up, and I almost fell into the people sitting in the seats across from me. I saved myself just in time.

Kristy Thomas, who rides the bus with me and gets off at the same stop, started to grin.

1

(Okay, okay, Kristy is the neighbor I was talking about, although she's not the owner of the cars with names, just related to the owners.) "I think this thing sounds like it has a cold. Or the flu."

"Or asthma and major allergies," I added as the bus coughed a few times. We made a quick exit and the bus made a slow turn around the corner and out of sight.

Not surprisingly, Kristy didn't say anything. Kristy is a bossy beast, but she is polite. Just like all the rest of the Stoneybrookians. Which means she is not going to comment on asthma and allergies, since I am saddled with both. Life makes me sneeze.

Good thing it makes me laugh, too.

"I'm going to name that thing that just departed, that the Stoneybrook school system calls a bus," I continued. "Seriously. I'm calling it the Wheeze Wagon."

That brought the grin back to Kristy's face. "So I heard," she said.

I was on a roll. "This bus gets to the garage and it says to the other buses, 'I've got such a headache. I'm allergic to the roads, and what do they make me do all day? Roads, roads, roads. I wanted to be a boat, but does anybody listen to me?' "

Kristy started laughing then and we went our separate ways. She went to a nice big house full of a million people, animals, and even a ghost.

I went to a nice big house, too. Only it was empty.

Surprise, surprise.

"Honey, I'm home," I called, just like the old sitcom fathers called to their wives, before the wives got smart and got out of the unpaid labor of housework.

(So sue me. Housewives get no respect, no pay, and no tax deductions.)

Speaking of "r-e-s-p-e-c-t" (which is the name of a song by Aretha Franklin, in case you didn't know), I decided to put on some music. I am not musical the way my twin sister Anna is (in fact, in many ways I do not resemble Anna at all, which makes me wonder sometimes why we are twins), but I do enjoy cranking my music up loud. I like it to fill up empty rooms and leak out of the windows and doors.

Loud music makes me less lonely.

So where was Anna? Where were our parents?

Good questions. I'm glad you asked.

But enough about you. Let's talk about me.

I'm Abby. Abigail Stevenson. I am not a native Stoneybrookian as you might have guessed. I come from far, far away.

Okay, I come from Long Island, which is

3

not all that far from Stoneybrook. But sometimes it seems like another planet.

I mean I have things in common with the local flora and fauna, and I'm starting to make friends, but I feel like an alien sometimes. I talk faster, I walk faster, I think faster. And sometimes I say things that make people's mouths drop open and their eyes pop out.

My schtick is different. (*Schtick* is a great Yiddish word, isn't it? Yiddish is an old Germanic language originally spoken chiefly by Jews from eastern Europe, which is where my family is from originally.) Schtick, by the way, *sort of* means "the things I do that make me me."

I have a picture of me playing soccer on my team in Long Island (I was the star forward, the leading scorer, and the co-captain) and it's a blur. You can tell who I am, but I am definitely moving fast. What I'm doing in that picture (I remember that game well) is leaving the other team in the *dust*. Watching the defense scramble after me to try in vain to stop me. Scoring. Making their goalie hate the sight of me.

But the picture represents how I feel. A blur. Moving fast. And then wondering why the only people who are keeping up with me are the ones who are trying to slow me down.

I stuck Aretha in the CD player and cranked

her up. My homework could wait.

Walls of boxes lined most of the rooms. Although we'd had an interior decorator get the house ready before we'd arrived, and even though we'd delayed moving in just to make sure that everything was right, we still hadn't unpacked most of our stuff. Mom had plunged back into work even more vigorously than ever. (Her recent big promotion meant that we could move to Stoneybrook, and into a big new house). Anna had resubmerged in her music, particularly her violin studies, and I just haven't been motivated.

As for my father . . . he died in a car accident when I was nine years old.

So that's our family. Absent, mostly.

It wasn't always this way. When my father was alive there were only four of us, but somehow, it seemed like more. We were always cooking. Literally. My mom liked to cook. She had started training as a chef at this place in New York called the Culinary Institute of America. When Anna and I were kids she taught cooking at a local college. My father was deeply involved in environmental engineering and urban planning. (Believe me, Long Island could use all the environmental help it could get. Like it has this incredible stretch of land called the Pine Barrens that some people still want to turn into parking lots!) I remember my parents used to joke about designing an environmentally correct restaurant and building it in a tree.

Anna and I actually had a treehouse. For our birthday one year, when we were little, we held a picnic dinner in the treehouse. Dad lowered a bucket on a string — Anna and I "helped" — and Mom put the food in the bucket. Then she climbed up to join us. It was so much fun. Dad would laugh at anything, and the way he laughed, everybody else would find themselves joining in.

But that changed after the car wreck.

I try not to think about it. They said he was killed instantly. That he never knew what happened.

The truck driver who ran into his car got a broken arm.

After that it felt wrong to laugh. Sometimes it felt wrong even to be alive.

Mom never mentioned Dad's name after the funeral.

Neither did my friends. They were cool, they helped by just being there. But I caught some of them watching me, as if I were going to break down and scream. Or cry.

But I didn't cry.

Mom changed jobs. She became an editor at a publishing house. She worked and worked and worked. She commuted into New

York City every single day except some Saturdays. She stopped cooking. Suddenly Anna and I were on our own, and we learned how to order take-out food big-time. Mom hired a housekeeper who took care of the house during the day.

And then one day at school I started laughing at this really dumb joke that my best friend was telling and I suddenly remembered how my dad used to laugh all the time. I laughed harder and harder and I couldn't stop.

I couldn't even stop when class began. I had to run to the bathroom. The next thing I knew I was sitting in the bathroom stall laughing and crying and wheezing and trying not to throw up at the same time.

After that I went home from school. Just walked out. I told Mom and Anna I'd gotten really sick, and I stayed home from school for a few days.

Although my sense of humor wasn't ever quite the way it was when my father was alive, it felt okay to laugh again. Laughing, I could remember my dad, and think he might be laughing, too.

I felt alive again.

But our family still wasn't the same.

I looked at the cartons. Before we moved, Mom had sold or given away practically everything. We bought all new furniture, all new everything, even chests of drawers and desks. The interior decorator decorated our big new house and we moved into a completely new life.

I gave one of the cartons a kick. Mistake. The killer dust bunnies attacked me. All of a sudden I was having trouble breathing. I panted a little and took a couple of gulps of air. Then I hauled my inhaler out of my pocket. (Have inhaler, will travel. Actually I have two kinds of inhalers — a prescription one for when my attacks get really bad, and a regular one that you can buy in the drugstore for times like these, when I get a little short of breath.) I held the inhaler to my lips and took a couple of drags on it.

A few minutes later my breathing was back to normal.

I flicked Aretha off. I needed real company, so I decided to plunge into the high seas of Kristy's family. Even if only half of them were around, that would be plenty.

Sure enough, when the door to Kristy's house was opened by her little brother David Michael and his pup, Shannon, the noise rushed out like a tidal wave.

"Hey!" said David Michael. Then he took a deep breath and bellowed, "*Kristy!*"

"Don't yell like that!" Kristy called back.

I started laughing as David Michael shouted,

slightly more softly, "Okay. Abby's here!"

"Thanks," Kristy replied in her usual firm, commanding tone of voice as she entered the hall. "Hi, Abby!"

"What's up?" I asked.

"Pasta jewelry," said Kristy.

"Huh?"

"Emily Michelle and Karen and Andrew and I are making jewelry out of pasta." Kristy was referring to her adopted younger sister, Emily Michelle, and her stepsister and stepbrother, Karen and Andrew.

"Like rigatoni and bow ties?" I asked.

"Yeah. You know the names of all that stuff?"

I shrugged. Mom had been a cook once.

But she'd never let us play with the food!

I settled down happily at the kitchen table, and before the afternoon was over we'd decked ourselves out in pasta necklaces and earrings and Karen had made a "hairpiece" out of spaghetti. Creative, but not practical.

I didn't realize how late it was until I heard Kristy's mother calling, "Hey, guys, I'm home!"

"Speaking of which," I said, jumping up.

I said good-bye quickly and slipped out the kitchen door while Kristy's family converged on Mrs. Brewer.

The lights were on in my house and music

met my ears as I burst through the back door. Not Aretha. Anna practicing her violin.

"Hey, I'm home!" I called.

To my surprise, my mother entered the kitchen. She smiled. "I figured you were in the neighborhood."

"Kristy's," I said.

"Baby-sitters Club meeting?" Mom looked puzzled. "I thought those were held on Mondays, Wednesdays, and Fridays. And aren't they usually at Claudia's?"

My mom never forgets anything. This has made me an honest person. (The BSC is this club I just joined. But more about that later.)

"Just visiting," I said. Impulsively, I hugged her.

She looked surprised. And pleased.

I pulled back quickly (you don't want to spoil your parental units), and asked, "Can we send out for pizza for dinner?"

"Pizza?"

I looked up and there was my sister. It wasn't like looking in a mirror exactly. Sort of like looking in a, well, blurred mirror. I have long, dark, curly hair. Anna has short, dark, curly hair. We have pointed faces and brown eyes. We were both wearing jeans and big sweaters. I sported Timberland boots. Anna wore fuzzy slippers. She had her glasses on. I was wearing my contacts.

Mom has brown curly hair, too, but she wears it *extremely* short. Her face is squarish and her eyes are a dark hazel.

But if you saw the three of us together, you could tell we're related. And you could tell that Anna and I are *very* related. A second look and you'd figure out we're twins.

Even twins disagree, though. "Two pizzas," suggested Anna.

"Why?" I demanded.

"Because you're allergic to everything I like, including cheese," she said, smiling to show that she wasn't taking a poke at me and my allergies.

"Not garlic," I teased.

"Ugh," said Anna.

"Girls, girls," Mom said, shaking her head with mock seriousness.

She looked at her watch. "I suggest you work it out, order the pizza — or pizzas — and call me when it gets here. I have a little more work to do." She headed for her study.

Anna and I exchanged a glance. Oh well, at least we'd all be eating dinner together. It didn't happen that often.

We sat at the table and began our pizza negotiations.

CHAPTER 2

Kristy's little stepsister Karen calls herself a two-two. That's because she has families in two houses, her father's and stepmother's, and her mother's and stepfather's. So she keeps two of a *lot* of things, one in each house.

The Baby-sitters Club is a two-two, too.

Or two-two, also . . .

What you've got here is your basic three sets of two best friends.

I realized that at the club meeting the very next day. The BSC meets from five-thirty to six P.M. every Monday, Wednesday, and Friday in Claudia Kishi's room. There are seven members, plus two associate members, who don't attend all the meetings and who weren't there that day. Which left best friends Kristy and Mary Anne Spier, Claudia and Stacey McGill, and Mallory Pike and Jessica Ramsey.

Let's start with Kristy, since she's the president of the BSC, the supposed Queen of the

Great Ideas, and the squeaky wheel most likely to get the grease, and her best friend, Mary Anne Spier, living proof that opposites can get along.

This is what Kristy and Mary Anne have in common. They are both short (Kristy is the shortest person in the eighth grade), they both have brown hair, they have known each other practically their whole lives (and, in fact, lived next door to one another until recently). They each lost a parent when they were young. Kristy's father just walked out one day when she was six or seven; the next time they heard from him he was in California. Mary Anne's mother died when Mary Anne was a baby.

Now Kristy and Mary Anne both have "blended families." That means that their parents have remarried and they have stepsiblings and new lives (and even potential ghosts . . .)

Kristy's mother remarried not too long ago — to a millionaire, lucky Kristy — and Kristy and her two older brothers, Sam and Charlie (owner of the Junk Bucket), and her younger brother, David Michael, moved into Watson Brewer's *mansion*. Which is how Kristy acquired her stepsiblings Karen and Andrew Brewer. Then Watson and Kristy's mom adopted Kristy's youngest sister, Emily Michelle, who is from Vietnam and was an orphan. Nannie, Kristy's maternal grandmother (owner of the Pink Clinker), also lives with them and helps keep order in the chaos, which includes a great dog, a cranky cat, some personality-free goldfish (but then what goldfish aren't), and the ghost of one of Mr. Brewer's ancestors. Believing in the ghost is an option: Kristy's little sister Karen does, but then she thinks the woman who lives next door to her, and between the Brewers' house and ours, is a witch.

When Mary Anne's father remarried, he chose his high school sweetheart, Sharon Porter Schafer, who'd moved back to Stoneybrook from California after her divorce. She brought two kids with her, and one of them, Dawn, became Mary Anne's other best friend, and then her sister, when Mrs. Schafer and Mr. Spier got married. Mary Anne and her father moved into the Schafers' old farmhouse with its own barn, near the edge of town. Dawn discovered a secret passage in the house that might be haunted.

But now Dawn and her younger brother Jeff are California kids again. Jeff missed California and his father so much that he moved back. Dawn visited them awhile ago — and only returned to Stoneybrook long enough to realize that she wanted to stay in California, too.

It was a hard decision for Dawn. It was hard

for Mary Anne and her new blended family to reblend, too.

But lucky for me, because Dawn's departure meant the BSC needed a new member and fast. So when I moved to town, they checked out my sister and me and invited us to join the club.

Anna said no.

That surprised them. I don't think anyone's ever said no to them before. I said yes.

But I think I'm still going to surprise them.

Anyway, Kristy and Mary Anne are organized. Kristy is president of the BSC, captain of a little kids' softball team, Kristy's Krushers (I'm now the assistant coach), and a good student.

Mary Anne is the secretary of the BSC. She keeps track of when we have sitting jobs and where and with whom. She writes everything down in the club record book. She's never, ever made a mistake. Not once. She also has a boyfriend and she makes good grades at school.

Oh, yeah — they are both pretty stubborn, too.

But Kristy and Mary Anne are not exactly alike.

Kristy is the most outspoken person on the planet. Okay, maybe not the planet, but probably in all of Stoneybrook. Shy she is not. She is energetic and quick-tempered and her big mouth gets her in trouble sometimes. But it also gets things done. She's not afraid to try out a new idea.

That's how the BSC came into being. One day Kristy was sitting at home listening to her mother try to find a baby-sitter, one painful phone call at a time. Suddenly she thought, what if my mom could make one phone call and reach a bunch of baby-sitters?

The rest is history. Or *her*story.

Mary Anne is shy. Painfully shy, sometimes. Very sensitive. I haven't been around Stoneybrook or the BSC that long, but I figured that out in a flash. She blushes deeply at little things. Tears fill her eyes over sad commercials on television. This would drive me crazy, but I see the up side of it. Mary Anne does not recklessly trample your feelings the way Kristy sometimes does. She's an excellent listener and from what I've seen, a loyal friend. I don't think she'd ever deliberately hurt someone else's feelings. It's too easy for her to put herself in the other person's place and imagine just how bad he or she might feel.

Perhaps these are the qualities that put Mary Anne ahead of the rest of the club, boyfriend-wise. She was the first to turn up with a steady guy. His name's Logan and Mary Anne thinks he looks just like her favorite star, Cam Geary.

Maybe. But he is pretty cute, and unique. He's a jock, like me, totally into sports. But he's also an associate member of the BSC. That means he takes jobs when we can't and that he comes to the meetings sometimes. Interesting, right? And cool.

So there's your first set of best friends.

Set #2: Another study in opposites in, oh, so many ways.

Claudia Kishi and Stacey McGill. Two knockout *babes*. This is what the guys in my school on Long Island would call them. They would be right. Not only are Claudia and Stacey easy on the eye, but they know what to wear and how to wear it. Fashion sense to the max. But each in her own way.

Claudia is the vice-president of the BSC because she is one of the founding members, with Mary Anne and Kristy, and because she has her own phone line in her room. That means BSC business doesn't tie up a telephone line another family member might want to use. Her room is also BSC headquarters.

Claudia has long black hair, creamy perfect skin, brown eyes, and a passion for art, junk food, and Nancy Drew books. She brings her artistic talents to her style of dress — she even makes a lot of her own jewelry — and looks great in combinations of colors and styles that no one else would be caught dead in.

She loves junk food and at every BSC meeting produces excellent sugary and salty treats from hiding places all around her room, including a hollowed-out book. Today, for example, we were eating Dove chocolates, barbecue potato chips, and pretzels.

Claudia also loves to read Nancy Drew books, which is a mystery to her parents. (That's a joke — see?) Her mother is a librarian and Claudia's older sister is a real, live genius, so I guess her parents think Claudia should read books such as *War and Peace* for fun. But apart from Nancy Drew, Claudia doesn't like books, or anything to do with school. She has trouble with every subject, basically, except art.

Claudia's an art genius, not an academic one. No doubt her parents will catch on sooner or later.

Now stop me if these two friends don't sound totally different.

Stacey, Claudia's BF (best friend), is the treasurer of the BSC because she is a math whiz (as well as a good student in general.) She's from New York and most of the time looks as if she were a model who stepped off a fashion designer's runway. She has shoulder length blonde hair, blue eyes with dark lashes, pierced ears, and a way about her. She's from

New York City originally, and probably the other members of the BSC think she is the most sophisticated of them. True, she is, at least in the way she dresses and views the world. But from what I've scoped out, she makes some pretty unsophisticated choices. For instance, recently she almost quit the BSC altogether, because she was hanging out with a way cool crowd. The kind of crowd that's too cool to be real friends, which of course you only find out when you need a real friend.

Fortunately, Stacey came to her senses and now she's back with the BSC.

Stacey was eating the pretzels. She was the *only* one eating the pretzels. Because she's a diabetic and her body can't handle sugar, she has to be very, very careful about what she eats and when. She even has to give herself injections of insulin every day. If she doesn't do all that, she could become very, very sick, and even go into a coma.

She doesn't seem to miss junk food. She can watch her best friend consume amazing quantities of it with amazing calm.

Now to the junior officers: Mal and Jessi, who are both in sixth grade at SMS. As junior officers, they can't baby-sit at night, except in their own homes, so they take a lot of afternoon jobs. Shared interests: books, especially mysteries and books about horses; also horses, and, of course, kids. (The #1 requirement for being in the BSC!)

Differences: Mal comes from a large family. She has seven siblings, including brothers who are triplets. She has curly red hair and blue eyes, and freckles across her nose. She wears braces and glasses and wants to be a children's book writer and illustrator when she grows up. She's already won a writing contest and she's secretary of her class at SMS.

Jessi has black hair, which she often wears pulled back in a bun. She has dark brown eyes and medium brown skin and she walks with the grace of a ballerina.

In case you haven't figured it out, Jessi is a ballet dancer. She takes special classes two afternoons a week, gets up every morning at 5:29 to practice at the barre in the basement of her family's house, and has had big roles in at least two ballets (*The Nutcracker* was one).

Jessi's family may be a bit larger than average: She has a younger sister and a baby brother, plus an aunt who lives with them. But it is definitely not as large as Mal's.

Have I left anyone out? Oh. Shannon. Shannon does not fit into the best friend theme. She is an associate member, like Logan, and isn't particularly tight with any one BSC member. Shannon is a neighbor of Kristy's and mine. She attends a private school, Stoney-brook Day School (where they have to wear *uniforms*). She has thick, curly blonde hair, pale skin, blue eyes, and high cheekbones. She has two younger sisters and a pedigreed Bernese mountain dog, Astrid, who is the mother of Kristy's family's puppy. Shannon and Kristy didn't get along very well when they first met, but they sorted it out. Then Shannon gave Kristy one of Astrid's puppies after Kristy's old collie, Louie, died, and David Michael named it Shannon in honor of Shannon.

I wonder if I would feel flattered if someone named a dog after me. Hmm. It would depend on the dog, I guess. Anyway, Shannon is really into school and is a member of all sorts of clubs, such as the astronomy club and the French club, which is why she's an associate member. Shannon can't come to every meeting of the BSC or take as many jobs.

And I can't leave out Dawn, although she's in California now and part of a new baby-sitting organization called the We ♥ Kids Club. I've never met Dawn, but from what I've been told, she's very cool. She's supposed to be very easygoing except when it comes to causes about which she is passionate, such as the environment (my dad would have liked her for sure). I look forward to meeting Dawn.

But back to the meeting.

Kristy sat in the director's chair she sits in every meeting. She looked at her watch. She looked at Claud's clock. She cleared her throat. "This meeting of the Baby-sitters Club will come to order," she announced.

Claudia pushed the BSC notebook toward Stacey. "Here. Your turn," she said. The notebook (another one of Kristy's great ideas) is sort of like a diary. In it, we write up a description of every job we take and also read each other's entries to keep up with what's going on with the many families we sit for. Very helpful, although I think I am in the majority when I say it is more fun to read the notebook than to write in it.

Stacey took the notebook and snagged a pen off Claudia's desk. She flipped open the notebook to a blank page and bent over it, her hair brushing her cheeks.

The phone rang almost immediately. Mal answered, took down some information, then said, "We'll call you back, Mrs. Papadakis." She turned to us. "For the day after tomorrow," she said. "Hannie, Linny, and Sari Papadakis from three-thirty until five."

"Can't. Test," said Stacey.

"Me, neither," Kristy said. She made a face. "Killer homework."

Mary Anne opened the record book, where

she keeps the list of all our appointments, along with clients' names, addresses, phone numbers, and special info about the kids, such as who has allergies. (If I had a page in the record book for my allergies, it would be full.) She ran her finger down the pages. "Mal, you and Jessi are . . ."

"Sitting for my family." Mal grinned. "I know." The Pikes always hire two baby-sitters because there are so many kids.

Mary Anne studied the book and announced, "The only person free at this late date is you, Abby."

"Sign me up," I said. "I like the commute." The Papadakises live across the street from Kristy and me.

Mary Anne looked a little confused, but she signed me up anyway.

Pushing her glasses up onto the bridge of her nose, Mal asked, "Have you heard that the art and music programs at *all* the Stoneybrook public schools might be cut back?"

This was not the sort of question that inspired me to leap in with both feet. Neither, apparently, did it immediately inspire Kristy, who merely leaned forward, looking interested.

Claudia, however, practically levitated. She dropped the Dove chocolate she was unwrapping and cried, "No way! You're kidding! How could they possibly cut the money for art? Art is important! Art is . . . we don't have enough money for art supplies as it is. I can't believe it!"

Jessi added, "Not to mention that dance isn't even included at all in the arts program. It's just as important — as the baseball team. Or the soccer team."

I didn't know if I agreed with Jessi. But there was no doubt in my mind that she worked as hard as any athlete I knew. Hmmm. I'd have to think about that.

Then I thought of Anna. Anna was totally involved in the music program at school. She was not going to be happy about the cutbacks, to say the least.

Suddenly the issue became very much more important to me. "So what's the gory story?" I asked.

"It's not exactly gory," Mal said, then grinned. "Oh. Well, the story is, the Stoneybrook public schools are organizing a weekend carnival at the end of the month to raise money for the arts program. Anyone who wants can have a booth, and all the money earned will be donated to the Arts Fund. My family's going to run a booth. We're collecting crafts from people, you know, asking them to donate handmade items, and we're going to sell them at the booth."

The word carnival sent the interest level soaring. "A carnival!" exclaimed Kristy. You could see her brain working furiously on Great New Ideas.

"Crafts," Claudia said thoughtfully, pulling on one of her handmade, papier-mâché earrings.

"I like it," I said. This was the sort of thing my family needed, I decided. It would pull Anna and Mom and me into the community. It would make new friends for all of us.

"We could ask *all* our families to have booths," said Jessi.

With a smile, Mary Anne held up the record book. "Not only that," she added, "but we have a list of people who have children — the perfect people for getting involved in a fund-raising carnival to support the school arts program."

"We are there!" I exclaimed. "Write me down. I can see it now: a big banner, maybe some lights: Don't be Heartless . . . and leave us Art-less!"

It took a minute, but everybody suddenly broke up.

Fabulous club. Fabulous audience.

Fabulous.

CHAPTER 3

"Achoo!" I sneezed.

"Do you have a cold?" asked Hannie. "My dad makes us special tea for a cold. It has honey and lemon in it."

"Or maybe you need a shot," Linny suggested.

Two days after that BSC meeting I was baby-sitting for Hannie, Linny, and Sari Papadakis. Linny is nine, Hannie is seven, and Sari is two.

"Forget it, Linny," I said. "No shots. It's just allergies. Animals make me sneeze and you gotta admit, you've got an animal or two around here." I was referring to Pat the Cat, Noodle the Poodle, and Myrtle the Turtle.

"Dogs and cats and turtles make you sneeze?" asked Hannie.

"Well, maybe not turtles," I conceded. "And poodles don't make me sneeze as much as other dogs because they don't shed as much." I looked around. Inside, it was nice. But outside there was more space with fewer animals.

"What do you say we put Noodle in the backyard for a little while and shoot some hoops in the driveway?" I suggested.

"All *right*! I'll get my basketball!" Linny disappeared in the direction of his room.

"I have to put on my sneakers," said Hannie, sticking out one loafer-clad foot.

"You go do that and I'll put something extra on Sari to make sure she stays good and warm," I said, scooping up Sari. Like her cat, Pat, Sari clung to what she'd been sitting on, in this case the throw rug in the den.

I disentangled Sari and took her upstairs to put on her red jacket and matching red cap. Then I took out one of the baby-sitters' secret weapons: the Kid-Kit. Another of Kristy's great ideas. Kid-Kits are medium-sized boxes filled with all kinds of things, from stickers to old books and games. Even though the kits contain mostly used stuff, they're a big hit when we take them along on jobs. That's because the toys and games inside are new to the kids we take care of.

We don't take them to every job, but so far, I hadn't left it home once, in case of an emergency situation. My Kid-Kit was a shoebox that my newest pair of soccer cleats had come in. I hadn't decorated it yet — the company's picture of the cleats on the side of the box looked good enough to me — but I had been filling it up.

"Mmm. Let's see, let's see," I murmured. "Let's find a toy for you to play with outside. Aha!"

Sari pointed. "Cat!" she cried.

"Cat," I agreed.

It was an old wooden puzzle in a box, six big pieces in different shapes that fit into a bigger square of wood. When the pieces were all in place, a white cat with black and orange spots and green eyes was looking out at you.

I grabbed one of Sari's blankets and we went downstairs and out to the basketball hoop above the driveway on the side of the house. I settled Sari on the blanket on the grass in the corner of the fence with the puzzle. (I had hauled my Nikes out of my backpack in the house and put them on. I'd sort of dressed up for school that day, but I never leave home without my Nikes.) I started shooting baskets with Linny and Hannie.

It was a great day. Sun. Blue sky. A nice cool breeze, but not cold. Autumn leaves blowing down and curling along the ground.

Noodle settled down on the other side of the fence from Sari and watched her and us.

It was fun. Linny's a good athlete and Hannie will be, too, if she keeps practicing.

I could have played all afternoon. Except for one thing.

My allergies weren't getting any better. I realized that the mold on the fallen leaves was probably getting to me.

No big deal, I told myself. Don't panic. Take it easy. It'll settle down if you give it time.

But the familiar, hateful tightness in my chest didn't go away. It became worse.

I jumped to take a shot and came down with a wheeze that made the old school bus sound good. I doubled over and put my hands on my knees.

It helped. Time to get out the secret weapon, I thought. I meant my inhaler. I was pretty sure the inhaler would make everything okay. Especially if I just took it easy.

"Abby?" Linny stood next to me, holding the basketball. "You okay?"

"Um," I managed to say. "Need my inhaler." I was about to ask Linny to get it for me. Unfortunately, I didn't have the chance. Maybe my face looked funny when I straightened up. I don't know. All I know is that Hannie suddenly shrieked, "Don't worry, Abby! I'll get help!"

She took off.

"Hannie!" I shouted. "Hannie, *wait!*"

But Hannie didn't slow down. She ran

straight into the street. *Straight in front of a car.*

I started running faster than I had ever run in my life knowing that no matter how fast I ran, I could never run fast enough. I couldn't get there in time. I couldn't save Hannie.

Then I heard the brakes squeal, and a horn blare.

And I saw Hannie dart safely into Kristy's front yard, without even slowing down.

The driver kept going, too. I had a blurred impression of someone shaking his head as he drove by.

"Oh," I gasped. "Hannie. She . . ." I felt Linnie's hand on my shoulder.

"She's okay, Abby . . . Abby?"

It was too late now. My heart was pounding. My head was spinning. I was gasping and coughing and fighting to breathe.

"Sari?" I managed to ask.

"She's on her blanket," Linny said. His voice sounded scared. "Abby?"

"Inhaler. In my backpack. In the house."

"You want me to get it for you?"

I nodded, gulping and struggling for air. "H-hurry!"

Linny ran inside the house.

I tried to walk toward Sari. I couldn't. I could only keep an eye on her from where I stood, bent forward, trying not to be afraid.

"Abby?" said another voice. It was Kristy. "What's going on here?"

I tried to straighten up, but I couldn't.

"She's allergic!" Hannie said, almost tearfully. "Kristy? Can you fix it?"

"Asthma attack," I wheezed. "Paramedics . . ."

Linny's voice said, "Is this it?"

"Yes," I gasped gratefully and grabbed the inhaler. I held it to my lips and took as deep a breath as I could manage. It helped. But not enough.

"Call for help," I told Kristy.

"Hannie, come with me. Linny, stay here with Abby and watch Sari," Kristy ordered. Kristy grabbed Hannie's hand and flew into the house.

I took another breath from the inhaler. No good.

Kristy told me later that the ambulance arrived in no time. But it seemed like forever before I saw the flashing red lights out of the corner of my eye. Then the paramedics were putting me on a stretcher as Kristy said, "Asthma."

"Has this happened before?" one of them asked.

I nodded and immediately he said, "This should help." He slipped a mask over my face and I took a deep breath. It did help, some. I stopped feeling so panicked. See, I told myself, I was right. No problem.

I left with lights flashing and sirens wailing.

Kristy stayed behind to call my mom and to take care of the Papadakises.

I thought, thank goodness Hannie wasn't hurt. I realized that my panic when she ran into the street was what had kicked a manageable allergy attack into a full-scale asthma attack.

I had seen Kristy's face as she turned away to take Sari and Hannie and Linny into the house. She looked worried. And shocked. The mask the paramedic put over my face to help me breathe looks scary, but it's no big deal. No way to tell Kristy that now, though.

Then I thought, there's something else in that look she gave me. But what? As the ambulance pulled away, I realized what the expression on Kristy's face meant.

Kristy was looking at me and seeing a sick person. An invalid. Someone who got sick on the job and wasn't able to finish it.

And Kristy was wondering if she'd made a mistake, asking me to join the BSC. After all, what good was a baby-sitter who got so sick so suddenly that she couldn't even take care of the kids who were her responsibility?

I took a deep breath.

"That's it," said a paramedic encouragingly. "Everything's under control now. Don't worry."

So I closed my eyes. And I worried.

CHAPTER 4

I know my way around an emergency room, okay? So although I was scared by the asthma attack, a part of me kept saying, "Been here, done this, no prob."

I'd had a couple of asthma attacks before, and a trip to the emergency room had fixed them. In fact, halfway through the ambulance ride I was already feeling better.

Emergency rooms (or ERs, as the doctors and nurses call them) are amazing places. All the doctors and nurses, physician's assistants and paramedics, are moving around at the speed of light, but with *extreme* calm. That's to keep everyone else from freaking out.

I didn't linger in the emergency room, though. I was rushed through to a treatment cubicle. A physician's assistant was already there, preparing to give me a shot. Her name tag said, *D. Ramirez, P.A.*

She rolled up my sleeve. "Epinephrine," she

explained. I nodded. I'd had it before.

She gave me the shot, then began checking me out: my eyes, my skin color, my heart rate, respiration, and all that other good stuff.

The medicine started working almost immediately.

"How are you feeling?" Ms. Ramirez asked a couple of minutes later.

"Boston Marathon, here I come," I answered with hardly a wheeze.

She looked startled for a moment, and then she smiled. "Tell me what happened," she said.

I told her about the disastrous baby-sitting job, and included a list of all the things I knew made me sneeze, just for good measure. "I don't know the names of all the plants and animals in the world," I concluded, "or I could tell you *every*thing I'm allergic to."

She gave me a quick smile.

"Abby?" a voice asked.

"Anna," I said. "My sister," I explained to Ms. Ramirez.

Nodding, Ms. Ramirez twitched the curtain of the cubicle aside and motioned for Anna to come in. "Try to stay calm, at least for the time being," she advised me. "You'll have to hold on that Boston Marathon until next year."

Anna looked scared and worried — and startled.

"Rats," I said. "Grete Weitz was expecting me. And Florence Joyner, too."

"Mom's on her way," said Anna, looking from me to Ms. Ramirez. "She has to come from Manhattan, so it'll be a little while."

"Well, we'll want to keep Abby here for observation for the next couple of hours anyway, just as a precaution," said Ms. Ramirez.

She wrote something else on the chart, hung it by the bed, nodded to us, and plunged into the controlled chaos of the ER.

My cubicle was in a separate room, a ward for the not-so-serious cases.

Anna sat in the chair next to the bed. "Kristy said she hopes you're feeling better," she told me.

"Mmm," I replied.

"I brought your backpack. Kristy made sure I got it so you'd have it. She said if you had homework, you'd want to be able to do it, even if you can't go to school tomorrow."

My eyes met Anna's. It was just like Kristy to be so organized.

I put my hand dramatically to my throat. "I'm sick. I think I'm allergic to homework."

"So what else is new?" Anna said. We laughed.

I pulled a book out of my backpack and read while Anna did her homework. Ms. Ramirez looked in on us once or twice. Finally we heard Mom's voice.

"And she's all right? You're sure?" Mom asked.

"A severe episode," said Ms. Ramirez, "but she responded promptly and we were able to head it off before it became anything more serious. What she needs now is rest and quiet."

"And no school tomorrow?" I asked hopefully as my mom and Ms. Ramirez entered the cubicle.

"I'm sure you'll be fine for school, as long as you don't run there," Ms. Ramirez answered with a smile. "I think you're ready to go but let's do a little test to make sure. Can you sit up?"

I could and did. Then Ms. Ramirez asked me to walk to the end of the corridor and back. She checked my respiration and heart rate. Then she said, "Can you say the first verse of 'Mary Had a Little Lamb' without taking a breath?"

I was able to. I even threw in the second verse. Ms. Ramirez nodded. She signed the chart and said to my mom, "You'll need to make arrangements to check out at the front desk. And then you can go."

"Great," I said.

Mom asked, "How *are* you feeling, Abby? No jokes."

"Fine," I said. "Tired, I guess. But fine."

We're not a very demonstrative family. Mom nodded and patted my arm. "Well then, let's get out of here," she said. She turned and went out to the desk to make the arrangements.

Soon we were on our way home (the hospital staff made me ride in a wheelchair to our car, for Pete's sake!).

I spent a quiet evening at home, doing homework and channel surfing in front of the television in the den. Anna came down from her room after she finished her homework and kept me company.

And you know what was cool? Every single member of the BSC called to see how I was doing. I mean, I don't know any of them all that well, but they all called. And whatever Kristy was thinking, she kept her conversation brisk and supportive.

Very cool.

Mom emerged from her study long enough to make me go to bed early. I argued, but secretly I was kind of glad. I was more tired than I cared to admit. I listened to the familiar and reassuring hum of the air purifier in my room and fell asleep almost immediately. I slept straight through the night.

The next morning I felt fine. Great, even. It had rained during the night and rain always washes a lot of the gook out of the air that makes me sneeze and wheeze. Standing at the bus stop I took a deep breath and said, "Ahh! Fresh air!"

Anna rolled her eyes at me. Kristy walked over to join us and said, "Hi, Anna, Hi Abby . . . Abby. You're feeling better?"

"I'm feeling great," I replied. "Thanks for calling last night. You know, everyone in the BSC called. I really appreciated that."

"Of course we all called," Kristy said, giving me a strange look. She cleared her throat. "So, do these, um, things happen often?"

"The asthma attacks? No. Not really. There it is! The Wheeze Wagon."

The bus groaned up to us and we got on. Anna joined some of her new music maven friends and Kristy and I snagged a seat near the front (away from the bus fumes).

"Like how often?" Kristy persisted. "The asthma attacks, I mean. Once a week? Once a month?"

"Not even that often," I said impatiently. I don't really like talking about my asthma. I'm still counting on outgrowing a lot of my allergies as I get older. People do, you know.

"Maybe a couple of times a year. I usually know when the attacks are coming on and I can head them off."

Kristy said, "You couldn't yesterday."

I shrugged. "Hannie panicked me, running out in the street like that," I said. I'd told Kristy the details of what had happened when she'd phoned the night before.

"But what if it hadn't been Hannie and Linny there with you and Sari? What if you'd been alone with a little kid? Or a baby? What would have happened then?" asked Kristy.

"It won't happen," I snapped. "Okay?"

Kristy is not tactful, and neither am I. Tension hummed in the air between us as we looked at each other. Kristy wanted to go on cross-examining me. I was daring her to.

At last Kristy said, "Okay. . . . Did you finish your homework?"

Truce. I accepted it and we talked about school for the rest of the ride. I couldn't help but worry a little, though. I knew I was a good, responsible baby-sitter. I knew that I could handle any situation. In fact, you could argue that I'd managed to handle yesterday's situation, in a way.

But Kristy was not convinced. And I didn't know how to convince her, except to work twice as hard and prove I really was a world-class baby-sitter.

I put the thought out of my mind. I'd deal with it when the time came. Besides, I'd resolved to not worry and to take it easy, at least for the day. No more asthma attacks for me if I could help it.

I told the soccer coach what had happened and skipped soccer practice after school. I went home early and actually did my homework. Then I got out my lucky (and falling apart) soccer shoes and began to rebuild the cleats on the edges, which were wearing down the fastest, with some goo-stuff.

Anna came home and stopped in the doorway of my room. "I figured you'd come home early," she said. "What are you doing?"

"Fixing my lucky cleats." I held up the one I was working on.

"I thought you just got new ones," said Anna.

"For practice," I explained. "These are for games."

"Why are they wrapped in that silver tape?"

"It, uh, helps hold them together," I answered.

"I don't understand it," said Anna.

"Most of my friends on the soccer team have lucky cleats. Or will only wear a uniform shirt with a certain number on it. Our goalie has a special pair of gloves that she inherited from her older sister who was also a goalie . . .

things like that," I said. "My lucky cleats and I have scored a lot of goals together. Don't you and your music friends have lucky violins or tubas or something?"

"I don't. I've gotta go practice." Anna turned abruptly and left.

I wondered if something was bothering her. Nah. I was probably imagining things.

A few minutes later I heard her tuning up. Since I don't like listening to scales, I put my headphones on while I finished working on my cleats. I danced over to the windowsill and put my shoes on it, cleats up, laces down to dry.

"I'm home!" a voice bellowed in my ear.

I jumped a mile.

"Mom!"

She laughed. "How're you feeling?"

"Great," I said.

"I stopped by Zabar's deli in Manhattan today," Mom said. "Tonight it's a deli picnic at the table."

"Great," I said.

When we were sitting around the kitchen table I decided the time was right to bring up the carnival. I hadn't mentioned it the evening after the BSC meeting because I was already practically asleep by the time Mom got home. And I'd forgotten about it in the unwelcome excitement of the day before.

"Carnival?" said Mom absently.

"To raise money. For the Stoneybrook public schools' Arts Fund," I repeated. I turned to Anna. "Like for money for the music program at school. For new instruments. Things like that."

"They shouldn't be cutting those funds," Mom protested.

"So maybe we could run a booth," I urged them. "At the carnival."

"Maybe," said Mom. But her enthusiasm wasn't overwhelming.

Neither, to my surprise, was my sister's.

"What do you think?" I asked her. "I bet all your friends in the music class could get behind this. Maybe even perform at the carnival or something."

"Maybe," said Anna. She stood and picked up her plate. "I better get to my homework."

"We'll talk about it later, okay?" I said.

Mom murmured, "Mmm." Anna didn't answer.

"Great dinner, Mom," I said, clearing off my own plate. "Deli belly delicious."

Mom laughed and shook her head.

I decided to zone out in front of the television for the rest of the evening. I'd just settled in with the remote when I heard Mom moan, *"Owwwwww."*

"Mom?" I called.

"That's it! That is *it*!" said Mom's voice from the hallway. She didn't sound angry. Just very, very firm.

"What's it?" said Anna's voice.

I jumped up and ran into the hall. Mom was standing at the top of the stairs, holding one foot in the air, massaging it through her slipper sock. Anna stood beside her.

"These cartons are not part of the interior design," Mom said. "I've unpacked my cartons, but you girls have *not* unpacked yours. I'd like it done as soon as possible, please."

Anna and I looked at each other. Unpacking cartons. Yuck.

"Okay, Mom," we consented.

We both knew we would put it off as long as possible.

"Why don't I believe you?" said Mom. She walked toward her bedroom with an exaggerated limp.

Anna and I burst out laughing.

CHAPTER 5

"We'll call you right back," Claudia assured the person on the other end of the phone line.

A meeting of the BSC had come to order. In between calls, gossip, and munching down junk food, we were talking about the carnival.

"My family is psyched," reported Jessi. "My aunt said her friend Mr. Major is a member of a group that dresses up like clowns and visits kids in hospitals. He knows all kinds of cool magic tricks and balloon tricks. Aunt Cecelia thinks we should have a booth with a clown theme."

"Everybody loves a clown," said Mal. She grinned. "The triplets want to run a dunking booth. You know, the kind where you pay money to throw balls at a target and if you hit it, the person sitting above the tub of water gets dunked in. I told them to go ahead. I'd be first in line to buy tickets and I had a lot of friends with very good throwing arms and excellent aim."

"Kristy's Krushers to the rescue," said Kristy, referring to her softball team. "But listen to this, guys! Watson's volunteered to rent carnival rides *and* hire the people who operate them!"

"Your stepfather is a cool guy," said Stacey. "That's great, Kristy."

"Now it's going to be a real carnival." Claudia held a Ding-Dong aloft. "Cotton candy. Candy apples. . . ."

"Well, I don't know about that." Kristy laughed. "But there will be a Ferris wheel, bumper cars, a whip, a tame haunted house, a fire engine ride. And Charlie and Sam and I are going to help out by selling tickets for the rides."

"Don't forget fortune-telling. The Kormans are putting up a fortune-telling booth," said Logan. He doesn't usually come to meetings, but he and Mary Anne had been studying together and he'd joined her for the meeting. He added, "I wonder if there'll be a kissing booth?" He looked at Mary Anne.

Mary Anne blushed and looked quickly down at the record book.

Everybody was so enthusiastic. I was glad nobody seemed to have noticed that I hadn't chimed in.

Then Kristy slapped her forehead, knocking her visor perilously askew. "I've got it!" she cried. "I've *got* it."

"Got what?" I said. I was kind of startled.

"You'll see," said Claudia with a grin. I found out later that Kristy's behavior was a not unusual prelude to her coming out with one of her Great Ideas.

"The carnival," said Kristy. "Don't you see? The BSC could have a booth, too!"

"Excellent!" cried Claudia.

"Decent," said Jessi.

"We can take turns running it," suggested Mal. "That way we can help our families with their booths as well."

"And have time to shop. I mean, enjoy the carnival," Stacey put in.

The phone rang and Claudia picked up the receiver. She took down the information and said, "Another rush job — the Arnolds for Friday night."

Flipping through her book, Mary Anne studied the schedule for Friday night. "Me. Or you, Abby. Why don't you take it?"

Kristy said, "I think you should take it, Mary Anne."

"Why?" Mary Anne looked surprised. So did everybody else.

Except me. I haven't been around this world twelve-plus years for nothing.

"The twins know you better," said Kristy. "And Abby probably isn't feeling well after what happened."

"Hey, I feel fine," I said. "That's the beauty of having asthma. If it doesn't kill you, you recover immediately."

Bad timing for that joke. Kristy frowned and said, "But I don't want the BSC to be responsible for putting too much stress and pressure on you right away. After all, you said it was the stress of the situation that caused your attack."

"Among other things," I said, fuming inside.

Mary Anne said quickly, "I'll take the job. If it's all right with Abby."

"I'm sure it is," said Kristy. Before I could say anything else, she'd picked up the phone to call the Arnolds back.

I was *not* a happy baby-sitter.

But I didn't want to wade in and start a war. At least, not yet. I'd give Kristy time to sort things out. If she didn't . . .

Then I'd let her have it.

The BSC meeting turned into a brainstorming session for the carnival. In between taking calls and setting up appointments we came up with a million ideas for booths, some of them completely whacked out (decorative trees made of junk food — that was Claudia's), some of them more reasonable.

By the time I left, I was psyched. I knew I was going to love working on the carnival and especially on the booth with the other baby-sitters. But I was also worried. My family was the only one not committed to the carnival.

I decided to tackle them again that night. Mom returned home late from work. Anna and I ate dessert (ice cream for Anna, ice cream made from tofu for me, since I'm allergic to milk) while Mom finished off a frozen dinner.

"Not bad," she said, rinsing the container and sticking it in the recycling bin (we only buy frozen dinners in recyclable containers). "With a little salt, a little seasoning, practically gourmet fare."

"So about the booth at the carnival — "

"Booth?" said Mom, as if she'd never heard of the idea.

"Mooom," I groaned.

"Oh, right," said Mom, leaning over to snatch a spoonful of ice cream out of Anna's dish.

"So what do you want to do? I'm open to suggestions. The sky's the limit!"

"No flying lessons, Abby," said Mom.

"Feeble," I said, making a face at her joke.

Anna asked, "Do we really have to do this?"

"We do," I said firmly. "Unless you think the school music program is not all that important."

"I see your point, Anna," Mom said. "Okay, the Stevenson family is in."

"Great," I said, with enough enthusiasm to make up for the dire lack on the part of Mom and Anna. "You're gonna love this."

Mom patted my shoulder and then swiped a bite of tofu ice cream. "I have a feeling we'd better," she said with a smile.

CHAPTER 6

Saturday

You will baby-sit for the Kormans and do many strange and unusual jobs.... That was my fortune on Saturday morning. The Kormans are working hard fixing up their booth for the carnival. They had some pretty good ideas, too. Wish I'd thought of some of them first!

Kristy arrived at the Kormans early to find them already moving at top speed. She said good-bye to Mr. and Mrs. Korman, who were on their way to a tennis date, and sidled around the huge, fish-shaped fountain in the entrance hall. The Kormans live across the street from me, in the Delaneys' old house, and I can see why everyone used to think it was pretty, well, ostentatious. (Check that out in your Funk & Wagnalls.)

So the fountain's still there, but it's never turned on now because Skylar (not quite two and the youngest Korman) is afraid of it. The rest of the house is a lot more comfortable and lived-in-looking, too.

I wish I'd seen it in the old days.

Kristy knew from Mr. Korman that Skylar, her older brother, Bill, who is nine, and her older sister, Melody, who is seven, were working in the huge family room in the back. When Kristy walked in, the room was full of empty soda bottles. Bill wasn't there, but he came into the room behind her.

"Here're some more," he said, and dumped an armload of soda bottles next to the wall by the sofa. "I reloaded the dishwasher with more bottles."

Melody nodded. Skylar, who was in her huge playpen in one corner of the room, screamed happily when she saw Kristy. She was clutching a graham cracker in one fist.

"Hey, Skylark," said Kristy, bending over and scooping Skylar into her arms. "What's happening, guys?"

"We're getting ready for the carnival," Melody replied. "We're going to have a fortune-telling booth."

"Great idea," said Kristy. "I wish I'd thought of it."

Melody said, "Yes," as if this were a matter of course. She didn't realize that she was talking to the Idea Ruler of the World.

"We're up to the fortune part," Bill explained. "We're going to write fortunes on pieces of paper and stick the fortunes into the bottles, see? Fifty cents a fortune."

"*And* a prize," Melody added.

"A prize with every fortune? Not bad," said Kristy.

"No! If your fortune says prize, then you get a prize. We're going to the store this afternoon to buy prizes."

"We're building the booth, too," said Bill. He fixed Kristy with a Look. "Only Mom and Dad said we couldn't do any sawing and hammering and nailing without them around, or someone grown-up. Are you grown-up enough?"

"I think so," answered Kristy solemnly.

"But let's write some fortunes first. Then a little later we can go outside and work on the booth."

She settled Skylar with a crayon and her extra-big coloring book and then sat cross-legged next to her to help Bill and Melody.

Kristy took a ruler and drew lines across plain pieces of paper. Then the three of them settled down to write fortunes on each line. They were writing the fortunes with gold and silver glitter pens.

"What about, 'You will get lots of presents for Hanukkah,' " suggested Melody.

"But what if you don't have Hanukkah," Bill pointed out. "What if you celebrate Kwanzaa or Christmas instead?"

Melody frowned. Then she said, "Okay. 'You will get lots of presents near the end of the year.' "

"That works," agreed Kristy. "Here's one: 'You will find the missing sock soon.' " She cracked up over that. Bill and Melody looked at her and frowned.

"Why is that funny?" asked Melody.

"Because *everybody* has socks that are missing. Drawers full of single socks that don't match. And they save them because they hope they'll find the other socks soon."

"I don't," said Bill.

"I like it when my socks don't match," added Melody.

Kristy looked at Melody's feet and realized it was true. One of Melody's ankles was encased in a lime-green sock and the other in a lavender sock.

"Well, it's funny anyway," said Kristy.

They came up with a bunch of fortunes after that. Bill created: "One night soon, you will stay up very, very late" and "Your favorite team will win its next game." ("I hope it's the Krushers," said Kristy.) Melody's favorite was, "You will discover a new flavor of ice cream."

Just as they were running out of fortune-telling steam, the doorbell rang.

"I'll get it," said Bill. He jumped up. A minute later, he returned with Druscilla following him. He looked a little surprised.

"It's Druscilla," he announced.

Druscilla lives next door to Kristy (between Kristy and me) with her grandmother, Mrs. Porter. It's just a temporary thing, while her parents sort out some problems. They're in the process of separating and selling their old house. (Have you ever noticed how when parents get "separated" the kids somehow get "separated" too? I mean, Druscilla's parents took her to her grandmother's so that she could continue going to her old school and not have her entire life disrupted by her parents' problems. But it makes her feel pretty unsettled all the same.)

Plus, her grandmother, who is a perfectly nice person, is not your usual warm and fuzzy grandma. Her house is a big old Victorian number that looks as if it's haunted. She even has a black cat that hangs out in the windows, giving everybody the mean cat eye. So it's no wonder that Karen Brewer is more than half-convinced that Mrs. Porter is really a witch named Morbidda Destiny — and for awhile was convinced that Druscilla was a witch, too.

All of this flashed through Kristy's mind as Druscilla walked into the room. So Kristy was pleased to see her. As loving and kind as her grandmother might be, Druscilla needed to hang out with some kids her own age, play with them, bury her troubles in kid stuff.

"Dru!" Kristy said. "Come in. We're working on a booth for the carnival."

Dru looked interested. "You're going to be in the carnival? What are you doing?"

Melody and Bill were a little formal at first with Druscilla. Maybe they were thinking about Karen's tales about Morbidda Destiny. And of course, they didn't know Druscilla all that well. But as they warmed to the subject of the carnival and their brilliant fortune-telling idea, their reserve began to melt away.

From there it was a short step to reading her their favorite fortunes. Druscilla laughed at all of them, and made faces at the gross joke fortunes that Bill had been making up. ("If your goldfish is missing, avoid sushi for dinner.")

"Try writing some yourself," suggested Bill. "We still need thousands and thousands of fortunes."

Okay, so Bill was exaggerating a little. But it was all the encouragement that Druscilla needed.

Looking far less self-conscious than when she'd first entered the family room, Dru sat down and picked up a lined sheet of paper. She thought for awhile, then began to write.

"Read some," said Melody.

"Okay." Druscilla held up her sheet of paper. "Beware the cold, cold snows of winter!"

"Oooh! That's a good one," said Melody.

"Are you going to have a booth?" asked Bill.

Dru shook her head. "No," she said softly.

"Why not?" demanded Melody.

"My grandmother can't do it and my parents are . . . busy," Druscilla replied.

Melody frowned.

"Here's the last batch!" said Bill, who had gone into the kitchen to check on the final load of soda bottles he'd put in the dishwasher earlier. He carefully set down an armload of clean bottles.

"Wow! You have lots and *lots* of bottles," said Druscilla.

"Maybe we have enough," Bill answered. "Maybe not. We've been saving all our soda bottles for days and days. I've been collecting them after school, too."

Druscilla said, "I can ask my grandmother if you could have ours out of the recycling bin." She added, "We always wash them before we put them in, so they'd be clean."

Bill looked pleased. "That'd be great!"

Druscilla ducked her head with pleasure and looked down at the page of fortunes she was holding. "I know! Let's decorate these before we cut them up and put them in the bottles," she suggested.

"I have colored pencils in my room," said Melody. "That'll look good with the glitter writing."

Soon the fortunes were in fancy dress, decorated with flowers and hearts and animals and bows and geometric designs and even drawings of footballs and baseballs and spaceships. When Bill and Melody and Druscilla were satisfied that the fortunes were as beautiful (and fortunate-looking) as they could make them, they cut the paper into strips. Then they rolled up the strips and began to stick them carefully into the necks of the bottles lining the room.

"We are going to have a super fortune-telling booth," said Melody, with a sigh of satisfaction. "I am going to wear a fortune-telling outfit. I'll tie a scarf around my head and another around my waist and my mother is going to make me a skirt out of one of her old fancy skirts."

"Wear lots of bracelets," said Druscilla. "And big earrings."

"Yes," agreed Melody. Suddenly she picked up a scrap of paper and wrote something on it. Then she rolled it up and pushed it into the neck of a bottle and handed it to Druscilla. "Here's a fortune for you," she told Druscilla. "For practice."

"For me?" Druscilla took the bottle and carefully removed the curl of paper. She unrolled it and began to smile a huge smile.

"Read it aloud," Kristy urged her. "What's your fortune, Druscilla?"

" 'You will help in a fortune-telling booth in the carnival,' " Druscilla read aloud. She looked at Melody. "Can I?"

"If your grandmother will let you," said Melody.

"She will!" said Druscilla happily.

Kristy was pleased. Druscilla needed to be included — in the neighborhood and in the carnival.

And it looked as if it were happening.

CHAPTER 7

In New York City and Los Angeles and places that have really big pollution problems from all the cars and the industries that dump their junk into the air and the water, some people wear these little white masks over their faces when they go outside to jog or bike or whatever on days when the pollution is really bad.

On Long Island I used to have to wear one of those masks sometimes when I played sports in the spring when the pollen count or the pollution index was high.

I was wishing I had a mask as Anna and I unpacked boxes after school one day. I was doing a fair amount of sneezing.

"You okay?" asked Anna, stopping in mid-box.

"Yup," I said. "It's not getting any worse."

"Look at this!" exclaimed Anna. "It's that teapot shaped like a piano that Corley gave me in fifth grade."

"A kitchen box," I said, "Let's take it into the kitchen to unpack it."

I began dragging the box down the hall. Anna followed, holding the teapot as if it were made of gold.

"Thanks for the help," I said, plopping down in a kitchen chair and pulling the box to me. Anna sat in the chair across from me. She didn't even notice I was being cranky.

"I wonder what Corley and Roxanne are doing. I wrote letters to both of them, but I guess they haven't gotten them yet." She sighed.

"They will. They'll write you back," I assured her. I am not much of a letter writer myself, but Anna's best friend since the beginning of time (or at least since kindergarten), Corley, was the queen of the note passers. She started sending notes to people in class the moment she learned to write.

As if she were reading my thoughts, Anna said, "I still have some of the notes she wrote me in first grade — big block letters on lined paper that say things like 'The teacher is a big meanie!' " Anna laughed, but she sounded a little wistful, too.

Roxanne, who was Anna's new best friend, (new compared to Corley — Roxanne and Anna have only known each other since third grade), was a music maven just like Anna. But her instrument of choice was the trumpet. She could really jam on that thing. She brought out the fast fiddle side of my sister, the classical violinist. Sometimes they would get together and make amazing (and amazingly loud) music.

"You should invite them up to visit sometime," I suggested. "Have them meet your new friends in the orchestra."

"Well," said Anna. She stood up and carefully wiped the teapot with a kitchen towel, then put it on the shelf. "I don't know anybody all that well."

"Yet," I said. "The key word here is 'yet.' You will. And think of all the people you do know — an entire orchestra. A baby-sitting club."

My sister smiled. It was a smile that said, "It's nice. But it's not the same." I thought of feeling on the outside of all the BFs in the BSC. I knew how Anna felt.

I reached into the box and pulled out a handful of silverware. "Ha," I said. "No wonder we have to keep washing the forks. This is where most of them have been hiding!"

We unpacked for another hundred hours, shelving books, and being amazed at the *stuff*. A million tons of cookware — really bizarre things, too, such as cherry pitters and olive stuffers and all these copper dishes shaped like fish and fruit.

"Molds," said Anna, holding a copper dish shaped like a cake-sized donut.

"Achoo." I sneezed.

"Don't you remember? Mom used to make molds in these things."

"Like Jell-O molds," I said, suddenly remembering.

"Some of them might be for cakes, too. I don't know. But they're kind of pretty," said Anna. "Let's put them up on top of the cabinets as a decoration."

We arranged the molds around the tops of the kitchen cabinets and admired the effect.

"Very artistic," I said. That's when I had my own Kristy-style inspiration. "Art food!" I cried.

Anna said, "What are you talking about, Abby?"

"For the carnival. Don't you see? It's a carnival to raise money for the arts program, right?"

Anna shrugged.

Undeterred, I went on. "So we bake up some cakes shaped like, oh, a violin and a paintbrush, and we sell pieces of it."

"Sounds hard," said Anna. "Mom has a lot

of molds, but none of them are shaped like a violin."

"But I bet you she could do it. She's got a million old cookbooks, too. And there's the library."

My twin did not share my enthusiasm. "You don't know how to cook," she pointed out.

"But Mom does. We can do the research and then she can just help us in a — a supervisory capacity. And, we can also make plain cupcakes and let the kids decorate them with frosting. You know, fingerpaint food."

"Little kids will love it. But it's going to make a world-class mess," said Anna.

"We can supply them with old aprons. Let's see. We'll need some of those tubes that you use for decorating cakes and . . ."

"Can we get to that later?" asked Anna. "Let's finish up here, first."

"Fingerpaint food," I said. "It's got franchise written all over it."

But I didn't gloat over my ingenuity. I joined Anna in unpacking nine million more boxes. Then we took a break from unpacking to take some of the best empty boxes to the basement to save for whatever. We decided to mash the others flat for the recycling bin.

"So we've done enough, right?" I said, doing the "I-Love-Lucy" stomping grapes dance on the last of the boxes. Anna, who had just run upstairs from the basement, laughed.

"You bet," she said. "But we forgot one."

She pointed to a small box in the corner of the kitchen.

"Sneak it into the guest bedroom with the other boxes. We can get to it later," I suggested.

"Let's just do it and be done with it," said Anna. She picked up the box and carried it to the table. Then she sat down and bent forward and cut the masking tape that held it together. "This is, like, an *ancient* box," she said. "The tape is practically crumbling. . . ." Her voice trailed off.

"Anna? What is it?" I jumped up. Anna's face was contorted. "You didn't catch one of my allergies or something, did you?"

Anna shook her head. She pointed down into the box.

I've seen too many horror movies, read too many of those books about things that jump out and get you. I bent over cautiously, expecting the worst.

It wasn't what I'd expected at all. It wasn't something from the dark side.

It was something from the past. Our past. I knew it, from the faint, familiar smell that wafted up out of the box as I bent toward it. The smell of a particular cologne . . .

Isn't it funny how a smell can make you remember a whole world? I froze there for a moment, and saw Anna and me. We were sitting at a table, a beat-up old table, no fancy hardwood table with a butcher-block top like our new kitchen table now. A birthday cake was on the table and its candles were still sending up little trails of smoke after being blown out. Paper was being torn and our mother was laughing and Anna and I were saying, "Happy birthday, Daddy! It's a surprise!" and I said, "It smells good!" and Anna said, "Don't tell, Abby ! Don't tell!"

Then Daddy held up the bottle of cologne. "My favorite," he declared. "Now and forever."

The box contained our father's things. After all the cleaning out and throwing away and starting a new life that our Mom had been doing ever since he died, there it was.

Full of things she hadn't thrown away.

My eyes met Anna's. We both wondered if Mom had forgotten about the box.

Then Anna reached down and pulled out our father's ancient Dress Campbell plaid flannel bathrobe and the faint scent of his cologne came wafting up with it more strongly. She held the bathrobe to her nose for a moment, then mutely held it out to me.

I laid the soft, worn flannel against my

cheek. Then I lowered it to the table and squat-
ted next to the box. "What else is in there?"
I asked, surprised at how steady my voice
sounded. "Let's see."

We found a pair of our father's glasses in a
leather case with his initials stamped into the
leather, and a big manila envelope with the
words *Woodstock 1969* written on it. Inside the
envelope was a ticket stub and a grass-stained,
mud-blotched, tie-dyed T-shirt.

"Wow," I whispered.

I reached in and pulled out our dad's wrist-
watch, remembering how he was always los-
ing it and then finding it again in weird places.

Anna held up his harmonica.

We found a college engineering paper with
an A+ written at the top, and a hand-painted
necktie with a peace symbol on it. And at the
very bottom, in a plain silver frame, was a
picture of Mom and Dad at their wedding.

"They look so young," said Anna in a
stunned voice.

She looked up at me, her eyes filled with
tears. "I miss him," she said.

"Yeah." I stroked the robe idly. "You think
Mom knows about this box?"

Blinking back her tears, Anna began to re-
place things in the box carefully. "She must,"
she said. "I mean, these are some of Dad's
favorite things. At least we know some of

them are. I bet the other stuff was special to him, too."

"Yeah, stuff from B.U.," I said, trying to keep my voice even.

"B.U.?"

"You know. Before Us." I smiled a shaky smile.

Anna managed to give me a small smile back.

We packed everything back into the box. Then I got the masking tape from the kitchen drawer and we resealed it.

"She must have forgotten," said Anna. "She wouldn't just leave this box of Dad's stuff around like that."

"She probably did forget," I agreed. Then a sudden gust of anger shook me. "How *could* she?" I cried.

It had hurt so much opening that box without warning.

Anna didn't answer. I didn't expect her to. I didn't have an answer myself.

"Attic or basement?" asked Anna.

"Attic," I replied. "It's cleaner."

My sister nodded. I didn't add, "And Mom never goes up there." I didn't have to.

We're twins. We knew. We knew we wanted to put the box away in a safe place. We knew we weren't going to tell Mom about finding it. It was our secret. At least for now.

Until we weren't quite so angry with her for forgetting the box and letting us find it like that.

I wondered if the smell of our father's cologne would linger very long in the kitchen.

I wondered if Mom would notice.

Or had she forgotten that, too?

CHAPTER 8

Thursday

This carnival has inspired everybody. But I didn't realize just how inspiring it was until I baby-sat for Carolyn and Marilyn Arnold. I think it is safe to say that nobody in the carnival is going to have a booth quite like theirs.

Mary Anne is a longtime fan of the Arnold twins, and they're pretty fond of her, too. After all, Mary Anne is the one who introduced them to Elvira Stone, the goat who lives on the Stones' farm near Mary Anne's and the Arnolds'.

So Mary Anne is, in a way, responsible for the Arnolds' idea for their booth.

"Mary Anne, Mary Anne, Mary Anne!" The Arnolds, who do not often scream, were nevertheless speaking *very* loudly and enthusiastically as they hurled themselves toward Mary Anne when she arrived to baby-sit.

That was a surprise. Another surprise was that the twins were dressed alike.

The Arnold twins, who are eight and in second grade at Stoneybrook Elementary School, look exactly alike. They have brown, bowl-cut hair, and brown eyes, and they both wear silver rings on their right pinkies and beaded I.D. bracelets on their left wrists. The only noticeable differences are that Carolyn has shorter hair and a tiny mole under her left eye, and Marilyn has a tiny mole under her right eye, like mirror images. But they do not dress alike. They used to, but not anymore.

Until that day.

They were wearing blue denim work shirts, overalls, and black high-top sneakers. Carolyn had tied a red kerchief around her neck. Marilyn was waving hers like a flag.

"Hi, you two," said Mary Anne. "What's up?"

Behind her, Mrs. Arnold laughed. "You'll see! And it's okay for them to use the Polaroid camera." She reviewed the standard "the-numbers-for-emergencies-and-where-to-reach-me-are-on-the-fridge" drill. Then she gave each of the girls a hug and hurried out the door in a jingle of jewelry.

"So, what is it?" Mary Anne asked. "You look like farmers!"

Marilyn looked very surprised. "How did you guess?"

Carolyn said, "We're *supposed* to look like farmers, Marilyn."

"You're going to become farmers?" asked Mary Anne, pretending to be very surprised herself.

"No!" Marilyn and Carolyn answered at the same time and burst into gales of giggles.

When they'd stopped laughing, Carolyn explained, "It's for our booth at the fair. We thought of it and our parents said it was okay if Mrs. Stone said it was okay, so — "

" — can we go and visit Mrs. Stone and Elvira? Please, please, please, you've got to or I'll go out of my mind," Marilyn finished the sentence.

"Hmmm," said Mary Anne. "Well, I think that can be arranged."

"Hooray!" Marilyn cheered.

"I'll get my notebook," said Carolyn. Carolyn wants to be a scientist and she often takes a notebook with her so she can "make observations."

"Will you tie my handkerchief around my neck for me?" asked Marilyn.

Carolyn returned just as Mary Anne finished tying the kerchief to Marilyn's satisfaction. Carolyn held up a Polaroid camera. "It develops pictures right away!" said Carolyn.

"I want to carry it," Marilyn demanded.

"Okay. Then I can make notes in my notebook," said Carolyn.

The three of them started down Burnt Hill Road. But Carolyn didn't make any notes along the way. Both she and Marilyn were too busy describing their great idea for their booth.

When Mary Anne heard it, she had to admit that it was Kristy-class. She just wondered if Mrs. Stone would think so, too.

They reached the Stones' farm, passing a late season vegetable garden complete with a scarecrow dressed in overalls very similar to the twins'. As usual, chickens were pecking around outside the barn. Beyond was a pigpen and a field where cows were grazing.

Mrs. Stone had on overalls, too. She also

wore heavy gloves and was carrying what looked like a big pair of pliers.

"Hi," called Mary Anne as they walked into the farmyard. "I hope we didn't come at a bad time."

"A very good time," said Mrs. Stone, smiling and pushing back the brim of her cap. "I just finished fixing the wire on the gate to the pasture. Time to take a break."

She looked at the twins and smiled. "I bet you've come to see Elvira."

"How did you know?" asked Marilyn. "Could you tell by the way we're dressed?"

"N-noo. But you two and Elvira really hit it off the last time you came to visit."

"We don't just want to visit," said Carolyn. "We have something very, very important to ask you."

Mrs. Stone led the way to Elvira's pen. "Go ahead," she said. "What is it?"

"We want to borrow Elvira," said Carolyn.

"It's for a very, very good cause," added Marilyn. "Please?"

"You should explain why," suggested Mary Anne.

"Oh. For the carnival," said Marilyn. "The one to raise money to pay for the Arts Fund so we can have music and art at school."

"For all the schools in Stoneybrook," corrected Carolyn.

"I've heard about the carnival," said Mrs. Stone. "But how can Elvira help?"

"We want her for our booth." Marilyn held up the camera. "We want to take people's pictures with her."

"And we're going to bake special goat cookies to sell," Carolyn continued. "Goat-shaped cookies. For people. We were going to make cookies out of oats for Elvira, but the veterinarian, Dr. Smith, said that that would be bad for a goat."

Marilyn nodded solemnly. "She said that it could make Elvira very, very sick to eat even too much of the food she was used to. It could even kill her!"

"That's true," said Mrs. Stone, smiling. "It's why I'm very careful never to let any of Elvira's visitors feed her more than just a small amount of her regular food. And I feed her a little less at her regular feeding times when I do. I don't want a sick goat — or a fat one, either!"

The girls nodded solemnly, their eyes fixed on Mrs. Stone.

"You've done your homework," said Mrs. Stone, both amused and impressed. The four of them had reached Elvira's pen. Elvira, one of the cutest animals on earth, and one who knew it, trotted over immediately to have her head scratched.

"Well," said Mrs. Stone, "that is some idea!"

Marilyn and Carolyn looked at her anxiously.

Slowly Mrs. Stone smiled. "I don't see why not. As long as it's okay to have a goat at the carnival . . ."

"Our mother called and asked," said Carolyn triumphantly. "The carnival's going to be at the old fairgrounds at the edge of town. So Elvira will be just fine!"

"Well, I think Elvira would love it. I've got a portable pen around here somewhere. I can bring it and Elvira and some hay and so forth to the carnival and then I can stay and help out, too."

"That's great!" Marilyn exclaimed.

"Thank you, thank you, thank you," said Carolyn. She held up the camera. "We brought the camera so we could practice."

"Well," said Mrs. Stone, "let's fire away."

It didn't take much practice. Elvira was a natural. Mrs. Stone took out her kerchief, which was blue, and tied it around Elvira's neck. Mary Anne took pictures of Marilyn and Carolyn with Elvira, and then of the two of them together, and then of Mrs. Stone and the twins with Elvira.

Elvira was a pro, chewing on a wisp of hay through the whole thing.

The pictures were pretty cute, too. "Excellent advertisements," said Mrs. Stone, holding one of them up. "You can put them on your sign outside the booth."

"Our sign!" Marilyn looked stricken. "We haven't even made that yet! And we've got to make cookies, too. We'd better get going."

"You still have plenty of time," Mary Anne assured her. "You don't have to do everything today."

But the twins insisted it was time to go. "I'll tell Mrs. Arnold," Mary Anne called as they practically dragged her away. "Thank you!"

She and Marilyn and Carolyn made it home in record time. Soon after, they were in the kitchen, going to work on the first batch of Goat Cookies. They twins had a cookie cutter that was in the shape of the head of a dog with pricked-up ears. On each cookie, the twins painstakingly redesigned the ears, dividing them into one round part and one pointed part, to look like goat horns.

"Beautiful," said Marilyn when the first batch of cookies came out of the oven.

Mary Anne had to admit that they did sort of look like goats' heads.

Mary Anne put them aside to cool. "When they're cool, after your mother gets home," she told the twins, "put them in a cookie tin to keep, okay?"

The twins agreed. Then they set to work making the sign for the booth. They had just agreed on a slogan for the booth, "$1.00 to have your picture taken with the Cutest Goat On Earth," when Mrs. Arnold returned.

As Mary Anne left, she heard Marilyn saying, "Would you like a special cookie, Mom? Those are *goat* cookies."

And Carolyn saying, "And they cost thirty-five cents each!"

CHAPTER 9

Kristy said, "I am truly awed by the Arnolds' idea."

Mary Anne nodded. "So am I. But our idea is a good one, too."

It was an unofficial meeting of the BSC. Everyone, including Shannon and Logan, was gathered around the enormous picnic table in the enormous backyard at Kristy's house. We were working on the booth project. Our booth project was derived partially from my idea to make cakes shaped like musical instruments and partially from the Kormans' fortunes in a bottle.

We were cutting pictures of musical instruments and famous art pieces out of magazines. Claudia had also supplied old art books and I'd talked Anna out of some of her old musical scores and music magazines. We found pictures of famous works of art such as the Mona Lisa and all kinds of musical instruments and drawings of famous artists and sculptors and composers such as Beethoven. We cut out musical notes and bits of scores from the sheet music Anna had given me. We were careful to cut everything into squares. We glued the pictures onto square pieces of cardboard. Then we laminated the cutouts and glued pins from a crafts store onto the cardboard: instant pins.

We would ask people to donate one dollar each for the pins. To make it more interesting, some of the buyers would also win prizes. We put an "x" on the back of each pin that was worth a prize.

The prizes? Hours of free baby-sitting, of course.

It was a great afternoon and we were having fun. Claudia was the pinhead (that's a joke, get it?), the boss of all the pinmakers. Meanwhile, Sam and Charlie were constructing a square booth using scraps of lumber.

Karen, Andrew, David Michael, and Emily Michelle were helping, too. Karen and David Michael took a keen interest in the building process. Karen felt that she was something of an expert, since she and her two best friends had "built" the castle (also known as a playhouse) out of old wooden crates and flowerpots and leftover wallpaper that now stood by the gardening shed at the edge of the yard.

"What color are you going to paint it?"

Karen asked. "There are buckets of paint in the gardening shed. You should paint it a beautiful color."

"Karen's right," Shannon said solemnly. "Color is a very important sales tool."

"As well as an artistic statement," agreed Claudia.

The rest of us looked startled. Except of course for Karen.

"I will *review* the colors in the shed and let you know what your selection is," she said.

Although Karen is only seven, she has, I have already discovered, a way with words and a big, *colorful* imagination. For instance, the ditch around the castle is not a ditch, it is a moat. What castle would be complete without a moat?

Halfway across the yard to the gardening shed, Karen stopped. Then she said to David Michael, "Could you bring some crayons and paper? We will take them to the paint showroom. Then we can make color samples so people can choose."

A few minutes later, David Michael and Karen, designers and interior decorators, had disappeared into the gardening shed/paint showroom. Meanwhile, Emily, who had been given a magazine of her very own, was systematically demolishing it. She was helped in this by Shannon the puppy. Emily Michelle would color on a page for awhile, grow tired of that, rip out a page, and hold it up. She'd let it go and the wind would swirl it away.

That was the cue for Shannon (the puppy) to chase it down, barking. When she caught the paper, she pounced on it. Then she brought it back to Emily Michelle. Sometimes Emily would take the paper and let it go again. Sometimes one of us, since Emily was sitting on the ground on a blanket next to the table, would reach down and snag the paper and put it in the bag we were using to collect litter.

I found a photograph of an accordion. Logan cut out a photograph of a rock star in the middle of a baseball stadium, singing the national anthem before a game. Then Mary Anne found a picture of a woman with long braids wearing horns, singing on a stage. Then I discovered a photograph of Jessye Norman, a famous opera singer. She was with James Galway, who was holding his flute.

Shannon (the person) cut out photographs of murals from the walls of buildings in New York City. Stacey even recognized one of the murals, from the side of a restaurant in the East Village. There were photographs of sidewalk art shows in San Francisco and authors at book signings and a woman with a blowtorch making a sculpture in a park in Seattle and dancers performing on the streets of Atlanta. We found pictures of musicians playing in a funeral procession of a fellow musician in New Orleans.

"It's amazing," said Kristy. "I mean, art is everywhere."

"*And* at least as important as things like math and science and social studies," said Claudia, making a face as she named just a few of the many subjects she does *not* like in school.

We laughed, but it was true.

"Aha!" Jessi exclaimed. She held up the word "article" that she had just cut out of a magazine. Neatly, she snipped the piece of paper in half between the "t" and the "i." She threw away the end of the word.

"A button that says 'Art'!" said Mal. "Excellent."

"I know," said Jessi with a grin.

Just then the two designer/interior decorators returned from the paint showroom. "The news is not good, I'm afraid," said Karen, coming to a stop before us.

David Michael shook his head. He held up a handful of colored paper scraps.

"Not good," he echoed.

"We have *many* colors for you to choose from," Karen went on. "But *alas*, supplies are *very* limited."

"Like we might paint ourselves into a corner?" I couldn't help asking.

Karen frowned, but she didn't answer me. She turned to David Michael. "My famous partner, David Michelangelo, will explain it all for you."

David Michael bowed. Then he said. "These are the colors: light blue, very, very green, pink, lavender, and yellow."

Even I could tell that those colors didn't sound good together. But Claudia was undaunted. "May I examine the color samples?" she asked formally.

"Of course," said Karen, waving her hand. "Be our guest."

With due seriousness, Claudia took the crayon-colored samples of paper and examined them one by one. Then she looked up at Karen and David Michelangelo and smiled. "We'll have a rainbow booth," she announced. "We'll make a sign that says 'The Arts at the End of the Rainbow' and we'll paint rainbows all over the booth."

Everyone loved that idea. Presented as a rainbow, the colors didn't sound so bad together.

"Claud, you *are* a genius," said Stacey.

"No, no," said Claudia, a pleased grin on her face, "I am an *artist*. And of course, I couldn't have done it without my consultants here."

David Michael and Karen gave little bows.

Just then the gate opened and closed. I looked up to see my sister walking across Kristy's backyard.

"Hey, you're early," I said.

"Our section of the band got to leave first today," said Anna. A satisfied smile turned up her lips. "We got everything exactly right."

"Congratulations," I said. I motioned toward the group. "You know everybody here?"

"Come make some buttons," said Mary Anne.

"There's room at my end of the table," added Shannon.

Anna said, "Thanks," and slid into the place next to Shannon.

"I usually stay after school, too," said Shannon. "For French club and a bunch of other things like that."

Shannon showed Anna what we had been doing. Anna laughed when Shannon held up a piece of sheet music she'd been cutting into buttons. "I'd like to try playing this on my violin," she said. "It'd be like reading aloud with every other word missing."

"Sort of the way we talk French in French club." Shannon laughed, too.

I looked down the table at my normally quiet sister. Suddenly she seemed to have plenty to say. Shannon, I remembered, hadn't talked all that much when she'd been at the BSC meetings. Not that Shannon was shy. At least I didn't think so. She was just more like Anna, not using up all her words at once.

I finished cutting out a dog howling and a little girl singing in front of a piano. Maybe, I thought, I'd buy that button myself.

I heard Shannon say, "*That's* a musical instrument."

I heard my sister laugh again.

Cool, I thought. Maybe it was the beginning of a beautiful friendship for my sister.

CHAPTER 10

Tuesday

Hey, Mal — how many pikes does it take to bild a craft booth for a art carnavil?

Okay, Claudia, I get your point. We were a little disorganized.

Hey Im not complaning. It was fun, a real chalenge!

Claudia and Mal were sitting for Mal's family after school. Since it was almost time for the arts carnival, Claudia wouldn't have been surprised to find that she was going to be part of the finishing crew, helping with last minute details.

But it turned out that she and Mal were more like the starting crew. When Claud rang the Pikes' bell, the door was answered by Margo, who cried, *"Mal-lor-eeee!"* and charged away.

"Hello to you, too!" said Claudia, stepping in the door.

"If it's more crafts, Margo, you know to bring them to the dining room!" Mal's voice called from the back of the house.

"It's me, Mal!" Claudia announced, following the sound. She looked around for Mrs. Pike. "I'm not late, am I?"

"No. Mom left just this second," said Mal. She pushed a strand of reddish brown hair off her forehead. "Whew."

"Bad day, huh," said Claudia.

"Umm. School wasn't bad, but this . . ." Mal waved her hand. "This" was the Pike dining room, a large room with carefully chosen "kid-friendly" furniture. Now, however, the furniture was barely visible under heaps of crafts: decorated boxes and knitted tea coz-

89

ies and beaded bookmarks and lampshades and patchwork blankets for babies and dolls and so much more that Claudia's head spun just looking at it.

"Wooooww . . . you must have a million things here, Mal!"

Vanessa, who is nine, had entered the dining room to stand next to her older sister. She said, "The whole neighborhood has been really good."

When Claudia looked slightly puzzled, Vanessa (who wants to be a poet and tends to speak in rhyme) explained in plain English, "We got everybody in the neighborhood to donate things. It's been awesome."

"You could fill up two booths with everything they've donated," Claudia said.

"I know," said Mal. "But we only get one booth. Did you know that every single bit of space has been given out for booths? Anyway, we've been assigned our booth space and told how big our booth can be. We've built the booth, too, but we still have to decorate it and figure out how to fit everything in. And how much everything should cost."

"What?" In spite of herself, Claudia heard her voice rise into the panic range. "You haven't decorated your booth? Or priced anything? But the carnival is in *three* days."

"I know. We're going to work on it today.

I figured we could divide into two groups. You could be in charge of decorating the booth and I could be in charge of pricing everything."

"A horse-go-round!" That was five-year-old Claire Pike, who had just entered the room with her eight-year-old brother Nicky. Nicky nodded.

"Yes," he said. "That's what we want. A merry-go-round."

"A carousel?" said Claudia weakly.

"We'll help you do it, there's nothing to it," Vanessa chanted, sounding more like she was leading cheers for Kristy's Krushers than creating poetry.

Claudia did not cheer up, not even when Claire and Nicky said, "We want to help decorate the booth, too!"

"Fine," said Mal. "Then Margo can help you and I'll ask the triplets to help me price things, since they're older and more advanced in math."

Claudia admired how tactfully Mal had arranged the tasks for her siblings.

But in the end it didn't matter how tactful Mal was, because the triplets, Byron, Adam, and Jordan, did *not* want to help price the crafts. They wanted to decorate the booth.

"Why do we have to do the dumb, boring stuff?" Byron asked when the triplets had been called into the dining room.

"Yeah," Adam agreed. "We should help decorate the booth."

"It was *our* idea," said Nicky. "Me and Claire. So we should get to do it."

Vanessa looked at Mal's face and said, "I'll be a pal. I'll help you, Mal."

"Thank you, Vanessa," said Mal, looking a little less harassed.

Claudia said, "Why don't you guys take turns working with me and with your sister? I don't need a bunch of people right now. We're still in the planning stages."

"Just help me get started sorting things out and then it will be easier to price them," said Mal.

"Not me," said Adam. "It's a big trick."

But Jordan and Byron didn't seem to think so. Mal ended up with Vanessa and two of the triplets. They decided to sort things according to crafts: potholders, tea cozies, mittens, scarves, patchwork, miscellaneous knitted and sewn crafts, and so forth.

It sounded good in theory, Claudia thought, as she led her group outside to the garage. But it wasn't a job she'd want to tackle.

The merry-go-round didn't appear to be an easy job either. She studied the booth the Pikes had assembled. It was your basic plywood and plank booth, with counters on three sides and a small door in one of the side counters so people could go in and out. Above the back counter rose three shelves.

"It's huge," said Claudia. "How are you going to get it to the carnival?"

"It comes apart," said Adam proudly. "See? Everything screws together and unscrews and packs down flat. Mom and Dad helped us design it and put it together."

"Oh. This is good to know before we begin decorating," said Claudia.

"Like a merry-go-round," prompted Nicky anxiously.

"Horse-go-round!" squealed Claire.

Claudia nodded, studying the booth. A plan was beginning to take shape in her mind. "Do you have big sheets of white construction paper? And maybe some ribbon that you wrap packages with?" she asked.

It turned out that the Pikes did — stacks of posterboard for projects, and spools and spools of ribbon. When Claudia commented on this to Mal, Mal grinned. "When you're in a big family, you buy in bulk," she explained. "It saves time, money, *and* arguments."

Claudia set up the decorating committee in the rec room. Across the hall she could hear Mal saying, "A potholder? I think it's a potholder. Put it on the sideboard with the miscellaneous knitted goods."

Claudia drew a series of big carousel horses

on the posterboard. She added poles at the tops and bottoms of them. Then Nicky and Adam and Margo and Claire (with some help from Claudia) colored the horses with colored markers and glitter, and made reins of bright ribbon.

Claudia was about to start cutting out the horses when Claire said, "These aren't real horses!"

"Neither are the horses on a merry-go-ground," said Adam.

Claire stuck out her lower lip. "But you can ride those."

"Well you can't ride these," said Margo. "They would *bend*."

Temper tantrum warning signs began to show. Claire's face turned red. She took a deep breath.

Then Claudia remembered Elvira. "You can't ride these horses," she said. "But guess what, Claire? When you get to the carnival you can have your picture taken with a goat."

That caught Claire's attention. "A goat! A real, live goat? With horns?" Her eyes widened. "Will he butt me?"

"She's a baby goat and she won't butt you. But she might eat a little hay out of your hand," said Claudia.

"Can we put a goat on our horse-go-round?" asked Claire.

"Um, well, let's make a little goat and we'll put it on the corner of one of the shelves," Claudia suggested.

The compromise worked. Claudia drew Claire not one but several carousel goats and Claire settled down happily to color and decorate them. Across the hall, the organizing continued, interrupted several times by the doorbell ringing as people delivered more crafts for the booth.

Claudia had just finished cutting out the last carousel figure when she heard a loud crash from the living room.

"Oh, no!" cried Mal.

"Byron did it!" said Vanessa.

"I didn't mean to," said Byron. Then he added, "I quit!"

"Is he going to have to pay for it?" asked Jordan. "I bet it was worth a lot of money. It was big."

By that time, Claudia and the others had crowded into the dining room. The floor was decorated with the brightly colored pieces of a terra cotta pot.

"Hand-painted," explained Mal. "Mrs. DeWitt's cousin makes them."

"It's probably worth at least *fifty* dollars," persisted Jordan. "Will Byron have to pay for it out of his allowance?"

Seeing Byron's face, Mal said quickly, "It

wasn't going to cost fifty dollars. And it was an accident. Byron, you and Jordan go get the broom and dust pan and clean it up. It's okay. Just be more careful."

"I'll be careful," muttered Byron. "I'm outta here!"

In spite of the smashed flowerpot, things looked a little more orderly in the dining room. Mal gave Claudia a rueful grin. "How's it going with you guys?" she asked.

"We're about to start the final stage — putting the decorations on the booth," said Claudia.

"As soon as we put these decorations up," said Claudia, "we'll come help with the crafts."

"Great," said Mal. "I've got a zillion blank stickers. We can write prices on them and then put the stickers on the crafts."

"Stickers," said Margo. "I want to do stickers now!"

"You do?" Mal looked pleased. "Come on, then."

When Claudia returned, she found Margo covered with price stickers. Of course, Claire then wanted stickers of her own. In spite of that, and in spite of more than a few disagreements over how much things should cost, the Pike booth was in good shape inside and out by the time Claudia went home.

"Good luck," she called to Mal as she was leaving. Mal sported stickers on her ears, her glasses, and the end of her nose.

"Don't worry," Mal's voice said cheerfully. "We Pikes will stick to it!"

Friday afternoon. Showtime. Time for the carnival to begin.

Kristy had waived the meeting of the BSC so that we could run our booths. Charlie and Sam had carted the BSC booth to the carnival grounds earlier, right after school. Mom had helped Anna and me take our booth there the night before and set it up. Our booth wasn't too complicated; we'd just used card tables and chairs.

Now, late in the afternoon, Charlie and Sam were still at the grounds, setting up the booth. Kristy and I loaded our stuff into Watson's car and the Brewer/Thomas clan headed for Carnival Land.

It was a clear, perfect day (perfect for people with allergies, too — hardly a sneeze on my horizon) and the carnival was an awesome sight. The huge old fairground at the edge of town was jammed with booths. Lanterns had been strung above the rows from one end of the carnival to the other. They flickered and glowed in the dusk. At either end, the rides beckoned invitingly.

"Everything looks great, Watson. Look at the rides," cried Kristy.

Watson stroked his chin. "I love those rides. Always have. A carnival wouldn't be a carnival without them."

It was easy to tell where Watson was going to spend his money — on tickets for carnival rides! He'd buy some of them from Kristy, who was selling tickets for the bumper cars. Bumper cars — perfect for Kristy, I thought.

Kristy, of course, had a map of all the booths. She and her family helped me lug stuff to my booth. Then the Brewer/Thomases and I wandered away to get an early look at the carnival. I walked with Kristy to the BSC booth to say hello to Mary Anne and Stacey, who were on the first shift. After Kristy decided that everything was running smoothly, BSC-style, she headed for the ticket booth at the bumper cars. I headed for the Stevenson booth.

I'd made a big banner that I'd hung above the booth. "Decorate your own cupcakes for the arts. One dollar," it read. I'd also managed to make cakes that sort of tied in with the arts theme. I'd done it with a little help from Mom's old cookbooks and a little help from

Anna. Mom had told me how to bake big, flat sheet cakes, then cut them into designs and stick the designs together. "Then you just cover everything with frosting," she told me. "Frosting will hide a *lot* of mistakes."

So I had made a flat cake that looked like a piano (sort of), decorated with chocolate and vanilla frosting. I'd made a plain flat cake and painted a pair of pink ballet slippers on top of the white frosting. After that, exhausted, I'd made a plain cake with marshmallow frosting and written the words "Support Art" on top in chocolate script. And then I'd stuck to cupcakes — dozens and dozens of vanilla and chocolate cupcakes. As the carnival opened, I took the last of the frosting tubes out of the cooler under the table, set up bowls of M&Ms and sprinkles, and put out some spray cans of whipped cream. (As an experienced babysitter, I planned to keep a *close* eye on those cans of whipped cream. I didn't want any food fights breaking out at the booth.)

I was incredibly busy in no time. Kids were waiting in line to put on aprons and decorate their own cupcakes. About a zillion proud parents took pictures of their kids and their cupcakes, although a lot of the cupcakes were eaten in a half-decorated state.

I cut chunks out of the big cakes and sold plenty of those, too. In fact, I sold out of those.

I realized I was going to have to make more (gulp) and I wished that Anna and Mom could have been there to help out, and to see what a success my idea had been.

A couple of hours later, when I was covered with frosting and whipped cream, I heard a familiar voice say, "Hey, it's the Cupcake Lady from Long Island." I looked up to see Jessi and Mal standing there.

"Did you escape from your crafts booth?" I asked Mal.

Mal shrugged and grinned. "It's the nice thing about having a big family. Plenty of volunteers."

"What about you?" asked Jessi. "Who's helping you out?"

"Anna and Mom," I said. "On Saturday. Tonight Anna has an orchestra thing and Mom's working."

"You're by yourself, then?"

"I am," I said, filling up an empty pastry tube with fresh chocolate frosting from the bowl in the cooler under the table.

"Why don't you let us do this for awhile, so you can take a look around?" Jessi suggested.

"Really?" I said.

"This looks like fun," said Mal. "I think I'd like to be the Cupcake Lady."

I didn't need any more persuading. A minute later I had slipped off my apron and plunged into the carnival.

Clearly, the carnival was starting out at top speed. It was jammed with people on dates, groups of kids hanging out, parents and their children. The carnival was *the* happening event in Stoneybrook that night.

I made a beeline for the bumper cars. "A dollar a ride, a dollar a ride." I could hear Kristy's voice before I even got close. "Three rides for two dollars, three rides for two dollars."

"One please," I said to Kristy.

"One ticket for the girl wearing the food," Kristy sang out.

I rolled my eyes, grabbed my ticket, and bumped my way around the ring.

It was great. Fabulous.

I jumped out of the bumper car, all charged up. "Thanks!" I called to Kristy, and took off again.

I saw people painting clown faces on kids, and jugglers and mimes from the nearby college theater department. Kids were playing Go Fish at one booth and musical chairs at another.

Then I followed a huge line to . . . Elvira.

No doubt about it, she was one of the *big* hits of the carnival. She stood there in all her glory, smiling her goat smile for the camera while kids flung their arms around her neck and patted her head and kissed her ears. She was wearing a red collar and what looked like a leash that was fastened to a stake in the ground just inside the portable pen. Behind her, so that it would be visible in every photograph, was a sign that said, "Elvira supports the arts program carnival." Mrs. Stone was sitting on an old milking stool in the background, smiling, while Mrs. Arnold helped the twins take pictures and collect money.

I thought about having my picture taken with Elvira, but decided I'd wait.

I passed many, many people wearing the BSC art pins. (I was wearing one myself — you know which one). I bought a fortune at the Kormans' booth from Druscilla. She read it aloud for me: *Amazing things will happen.*

"They already have," I told her. She was giggling as I left.

And at the Pikes' booth, I wasn't at all surprised to see Adam, Jordan, Byron, and Margo doing a brisk business, and wearing price stickers themselves!

I was still laughing when I returned to my booth.

Mal had frosting on the end of her nose. Jessi was wearing about a bowlful of icing with crumbs on the front of her apron.

The table was crowded with kids making

cupcakes and more were waiting on line.

I stood behind the counter again and told Mal and Jessi about the booths I'd seen. They hung out for a little while longer, and decorated cupcakes of their own. Then they took off.

But I wasn't on my own long. Before the evening was over, I'd seen every single member of the BSC, and they'd all given me breaks from my booth. Once, I traded off and helped out at the BSC booth.

The cupcakes ran out just before closing time.

I was a success.

And so was the carnival.

CHAPTER 12

With Kristy in charge, you are never on time.

You are early.

So naturally we arrived at the carnival Bright And Early the next morning. For soccer, I will drag my unhappy body from the bed at any hour. Stagger across a frozen, muddy field in the freezing wind at dawn to defeat the enemy. Arrive at the game hours earlier just to check out the field.

I would have said that would be the only way you'd get me to look at the early side of Saturday morning. Especially after Anna and I'd spent what seemed to be the entire night baking cupcakes, taking the last batch out of the oven just as Mom was dragging her weary self home from the office.

I would have been wrong. Fortunately, Anna is an early riser and she knew the plan. So she hauled my unconscious body out of bed, propped me up over the cereal, and prodded me along until we were both ready when Kristy leaned on the front doorbell at the crack of dawn.

Okay, not that early, but you get the idea.

I was on BSC booth duty with Kristy first thing that morning. Anna was in charge of our booth. Mom had gone into the city to work, but she was going to catch the 12:45 train and be back in Stoneybrook by 3:00 to do her time with us in the afternoon.

I helped Anna lug the cupcakes and fresh supplies of icing and toppings to the booth, told her what I'd learned from booth duty the night before, warned her against the perils of whipped cream in a can, and went off to join Kristy.

Kristy had five pins stuck on her sweatshirt and six more on her collie cap.

"I guess you're not hard to pin down," I said.

Kristy gave a snort of laughter. "That's terrible," she replied. Then she shoved a basket of pins at me. "Decorate yourself," she ordered.

Who am I to argue with Kristy Thomas? I decorated.

The morning crowd was quieter than the crowd the night before. A lot of the adults were moving along in a sleepy way behind little kids who were zooming around like pin-balls. The pins were not a big selling item in this crowd, although Mr. Papadakis's mood soared from weary to delighted when the pin he bought turned out to have earned him five hours of free baby-sitting.

He pinned it proudly on his jacket and pock-eted the certificate we'd written up. "Look at that, Sari!" he said to his daughter, who was in her stroller. "Let's go get some orange juice to celebrate."

"Juice," agreed Sari.

"Then can we go see Elvira, Dad?" asked Linny.

"Puleeeeese," begged Hannie.

Kristy and I looked at each other and laughed.

Kristy was working a double shift at the booth. Stacey came to take my place and I went back to check on Anna.

I am ashamed to admit what I saw, but I saw it. With my own eyes.

Fortunately, no one was around since it was still so early.

Just as I reached the booth, Anna squirted Shannon right in the apron with whipped cream. Shannon shrieked, then wiped the whipped cream off and flung it back at Anna.

"Hey!" I shouted, running toward them.

They both jumped like guilty little kids.

Then they looked at each other and started howling with laughter.

"S-sorry," gasped Anna. "It's just that Shannon said she'd never been in a food fight before and I . . ." She started laughing again.

"*Never* been in a food fight? Does your lunchroom serve edible food or something?" I asked.

Shannon made a tremendous effort and managed to stop laughing. "No. Is that what you're supposed to do with the mystery meat?"

"It's one idea," I said.

"Let's go ride some rides," suggested Anna, untying her apron.

"Okay," said Shannon.

"We'll be right back," Anna promised. I waved good-bye to them and served a few breakfast cupcakes to kids with indulgent parents. I wished I'd thought to make coffee and have hot tea. More people might have bought cupcakes as breakfast food, adults at least. Kids had no problem with cupcakes for breakfast.

Anna returned after leaving Shannon at the BSC booth. I decided I needed a soda. The crowds were starting to pick up — it was almost one o'clock — so I told Anna I'd be right back.

The soda booth guy had just handed me my

soda and my change when a voice on the radio behind him said, "We interrupt this program for an important announcement."

I didn't pay much attention. Newspeople are always getting hysterical about things such as presidential hairdos. Then as I turned away, someone in line said, "You know, those trains are usually so reliable. I wonder what caused the eleven forty-five to derail like that?"

My heart stopped. "The twelve forty-five from where?" I interrupted the two people urgently.

"New York," one of the men said. "It gets here at two thirty-four. Only I guess it won't today."

I whirled around. "Turn up the radio!" I practically shouted. "My mother was on that train!"

The guy in the booth turned quickly and raised the volume on the radio.

". . . from New York, which pulled out of the station and then, shortly thereafter, derailed. Police officers, medical personnel, and firefighters are on the scene. There was a small fire but it is now under control. The extent of injuries are unknown, although we have seen several people removed from the scene on stretchers. No fatalities have yet been reported."

"Mom," I whispered. I put the soda down

gently on the edge of the booth. "Thank you. That's all I want."

"I'm sure your mother will be all right," the soda man assured me.

"Do you need any help?" asked one of the people in line behind me.

I shook my head. Maybe Mom hadn't left her office yet, I thought. She probably forgot about her train. Yeah, that's it. She forgot. She's always forgetting what time it is.

By some miracle, the first pay phone I found was free. I dropped the change in with trembling fingers.

A voice I didn't recognize answered the phone at my mother's office.

"Mrs. Stevenson? Oh, she left almost two hours ago. Said she had a very important date. May I take a message?"

"No, thank you," I whispered. I hung up the phone.

I leaned against the phone for a few moments, trying not to throw up. When I looked up again, I was dizzy.

Stay calm, I told myself. Find Anna.

I hurried back to our booth and pulled Anna aside. I told her what had happened.

"You called the office," she repeated, just to make sure.

"She'd already left," I said again. "She told them she had an important date."

By unspoken agreement, we began closing up the booth. Then we headed off to find Kristy and tell her the news. Maybe someone in her family could give us a ride to the local train station. They might know more there.

At the BSC booth we learned that Kristy had gone with her mother to take Karen and David Michael on the bumper cars.

"What's wrong?" asked Claudia.

"Can't stop now," I gasped. "We'll explain later."

We hurried toward the bumper cars. As we pushed through the crowd I could hear myself starting to wheeze.

"Kristy!" said Anna, grabbing her by the arm as she came out of the bumper car ride.

I fished in my pocket for my inhaler. I held it to my lips and took a deep breath.

"Oh, no!" cried Kristy, running to me. "Another asthma attack?"

CHAPTER 13

The he inhaler almost always works if you use it in time. It worked fine this time. I took another breath from it, then folded it up and put it away.

"No," I said. I took a deep, slow breath. I forced myself to be calm. "No."

"You're okay?" asked Kristy.

"Yes!" I said impatiently.

"It's Mom," Anna burst out. "There's been a train derailment and it was her train."

"I called her office when we heard about it," I explained. "They said she left. And I know the train she was planning on taking was the twelve forty-five."

Kristy's mother hurried over to us. "Charlie told me. Come on. We'll drive to the station and see if they know anything there."

Kristy said, "I'll get on the phones here. We

can take turns calling when we're not at our booth. Your booth is closed?"

Anna and I nodded. "We left the money at the BSC booth," I said.

"Fine," replied Kristy briskly. "We'll meet back at the BSC booth. And we'll take care of your booth. Don't worry, guys."

"Thanks, Kristy," I said.

But when we reached the train station, no one was at the ticket window. *Closed Saturdays*, the sign at the window read.

We called the local police from the train station, but they didn't know anything. Then Mrs. Brewer phoned the local newspaper and the local news station. We also called the railroad line.

No one knew more than what we'd already heard.

"They'd know by now if there were any really serious injuries," said Kristy's mother reassuringly as we returned to the car. She didn't add, "or fatalities."

But that's what I was thinking.

By six o'clock, we were pretty sure no one had been killed. But that was about all we knew. We'd stayed at the carnival because that's where we were supposed to meet Mom. But Mrs. Brewer had driven back to our house and left a note on our door about where we were, just in case.

"Mom has a cellular phone," I said. "Why hasn't she called? She could use it to call from the train."

"I'm sure there's a good reason," said Anna.

Or a bad one, I thought. But I kept my mouth shut.

Like zombies, Anna and I packed up the stuff from our booth. All around us people were laughing and talking and having a great time. The carnival was at its peak.

We carried the coolers to Mr. Brewer's car. We were about to turn around to retrieve the rest of the stuff when I heard the most wonderful sound in the world.

Our mother's voice, calling our names.

"Abby! Anna! Oh, thank goodness you're here!"

We shrieked like crazy people. There was Mom, running across the parking lot, her scarf flying, her briefcase banging against her leg. I honestly didn't know Mom could run that fast.

Anna and I covered some ground pretty fast, too. It's a wonder the three of us crashing together didn't cause a minor earthquake.

We almost fell over from the impact.

"What about you? We thought you were dead!"

"Where *were* you?" cried Anna. "Why didn't you call?"

"Oh, Abby. Oh, Anna." Mom squeezed each of us hard, and gave us a kiss. Normally I would have pulled away. But this was not a normal time.

"Well," I demanded. "What happened?"

"You're not hurt, are you?" asked Anna.

"No, no," said Mom. "It wasn't my train . . ."

"But they said you'd left your office . . ."

"There were two trains," explained Mom. "Because of the crowds heading out of town for leaf season. I got stuck on the second train. And *it* got stuck in the tunnel behind the train that derailed. We couldn't get out of the train and the cellular phones didn't work in the tunnel. But I had forgotten mine, anyway. For awhile, the lights didn't work either."

"How awful," gasped Anna. "To be trapped in the tunnel in the dark."

Mom's lips twisted in a wry grin. "It was pretty bad. But not as bad as being on the derailed train. Anyway, after hours and hours, they evacuated us. We had to walk back to the station. And then they finally put us on a bus, and of course the bus had to make a million stops."

She heaved a deep sigh. "I knew you'd be worried. But I didn't know how to reach you."

"Well, you're here now. That's what's important," I said.

Mom hugged us again, then straightened up. Mr. Brewer patted her on the shoulder. "They've been very calm and brave," he said.

"Let's go home," said Anna.

"Home?" Mom's smile was shaky, but her eyes were shiny with enthusiasm as well as unshed tears. "I came to work in a carnival and *that's* what I'm going to do."

"Really?" I asked.

"You better believe it," Mom said. "Come on."

So the Cupcake Lady was back in business — only this time there were three of us. Somehow, none of us wanted to go wandering around the carnival without the others.

Kristy and Mary Anne came over and gave us a break so we could show Mom the sights. And, okay, so we could have our photograph taken with Elvira.

But we spent most of the rest of the carnival in our booth. The Cupcake Family. Can you believe it?

And it was pretty sweet.

CHAPTER 14

"Shannon says she heard the carnival was so successful that people are saying they should make it an annual event. She says people already want to sign up for booths for next year," Anna said, hanging up the phone.

It was Sunday evening. The carnival had closed late that afternoon. We'd spent the rest of Saturday evening at our booth, then stayed up most of Saturday night baking cupcakes and cakes. I showed Mom how I made the piano cake. And she and Anna and I had designed and made a three-layer cake that looked like an artist's palette. Pretty cool. Pretty delicious, too.

We had had fun. Just plain fun.

And I was tired. Just plain wiped out.

We were finishing a late dinner of what Mom called Sandwich Du Jour. That means "sandwich of the day" and it means that anything in the refrigerator is fair game. I was actually eating chicken dogs that I had nuked in the microwave, with baked beans and mustard mixed together.

Anna finished her sandwich and said, "Cupcakes, anyone?"

"Ugh!" I groaned.

Mom said, "I'm not worried. I happen to know we sold every last one."

"Yup," I said.

"It was Abby's idea," said Anna, "to make fancy cakes and the cupcakes for the kids to decorate. Fingerpaint food."

"Brilliant," said Mom.

"You gave me the idea," I said. "Or, I guess, those did." I pointed to the shining copper molds that were lining the space above the cabinets in our kitchen.

Mom looked up. "Oh! You know, I meant to tell you how good those looked up there. I hadn't seen or thought about them in years."

"Yeah," I said dryly. "And that's not all."

Anna knew where I was headed. She joined in. "Yup. We've unpacked all the cartons now. *All* of them."

"Except one," I added. "There's one more in the attic. . . . If you'll excuse me."

"I'll clear the table," said Anna.

Leaving Mom looking puzzled, I bounded up the stairs to the attic and returned as quickly as possible holding the box with our father's things in it.

I didn't think our mother recognized it even then.

"We, ah, found this with all the other boxes," I said. I set it down on the empty table. Anna cut the masking tape we'd sealed the box with such a short time before.

Did she smell Dad's cologne before we opened the box? She might have, because her face changed. For one instant it looked soft and young and smiling, the way I remembered Mom from when we were kids.

From when Dad was still alive.

But then the moment passed and she drew her breath in sharply and closed her eyes and put her hand over her heart as if to protect it.

"It's Dad's stuff," said Anna. "All kinds of things. Special things. . . . We thought you gave away all his stuff when he, when the accident happened."

"Why didn't you tell us?" I asked.

Mom didn't move. Didn't speak. Then she slowly opened her eyes and they filled with tears. Huge, silent tears that spilled over and fell down her cheeks.

"Oh, Mom," cried Anna. She leaned forward, but Mom held out her hand and shook her head slightly.

"It's okay," she said. Her voice was hoarse and very low. She grew silent again.

"Mom?" I said.

She seemed to be coming back from far away. Then she leaned forward and began to take things out of the box.

"His bathrobe," she murmured. She stroked it, put it on her lap, held it there. "Oh, Jon. I never washed it, you know. It was hanging on the back of the door when I came home from the hospital after he . . . died. I put it on. I slept in it every night for weeks. But then I realized that no matter how much I slept, I'd always wake up and it wouldn't be a bad dream. It would be real.

"And I realized I had two children. Our two children. So I put the robe away. I went around our room that morning just sweeping things into this box. And I took it to the attic and left it there. The next day I brought home more boxes. I threw away everything that was his. I didn't want to be reminded.

"It made me remember. And I was afraid remembering would make me weak."

"Did you cry?" asked Anna.

"Yes." Mom lifted out the glasses. "I took these to the hospital with me. I thought he might need them. I didn't know how — how bad it was."

I reached past her and pulled out the envelope. A sudden smile lit up Mom's sad face. "Your father," she said, "was at Woodstock. The first Woodstock . . . I wonder what he would have thought of the second one." She held up the ticket. "It's probably a collector's item now. He did always say he was probably one of the few people on earth who had actually bought and paid for a ticket to what turned out to be one of the most famous free concerts of all time. And that shirt. I tried to get him to throw it away. But he wouldn't."

I had lifted the watch out of the box. "He wasn't wearing his watch when the accident happened?"

She shook her head. "He'd been looking for it for two days. I found it in the drain cup in the sink that morning after he left for work."

Holding the harmonica, Mom said, "That's where your ear for music comes from, Anna. You remember him playing this?"

Anna nodded. "Of course I do."

"He'd be so proud of you both. Two is better than twice as much. That's what he said when he saw you, right after you were born. He could mix words around so that even if they didn't make sense, they sounded as if they did. The way you do, Abby. You both remind me of him so much sometimes, in different ways."

Her voice trailed off again. She stroked the soft worn flannel of the robe.

"You never talked about him after you told us he had died," said Anna. "I never knew why."

"I couldn't. I always meant to. But it hurt. And then when it stopped hurting quite so much, I was afraid I would start to hurt all over again if I did talk about him. It was like being in the dark in that tunnel and not being sure I was going to make it out again. And then I was so glad . . .

"But I didn't forget. Not one single day have I forgotten. I might have forgotten about that carton, maybe even deliberately.

"But never about Jonathan."

Mom looked down at the box. "It's time these things had new homes."

For one awful moment, I thought Mom was going to give away our father's things.

She saw my face and reached out and patted my hand. "Don't worry. I'm not going to throw anything away. In fact," she lifted up the watch and slid it over my wrist. It was big and clunky and heavy and old fashioned. I loved it.

"Thanks, Mom," I said.

She turned to Anna. "I expect someday you will write a symphony for violin and harmonica," she said, handing Anna the harmonica.

Anna clutched the harmonica, her eyes shining.

"We're a family," Mom said. "And don't you forget it, you hear? We support each other, we stick together. We talk."

Anna and I nodded.

Mom held up the bathrobe. "I have a place on the back of my bedroom door where this will hang nicely. And the picture can go on the piano in the living room."

She set the glasses aside. "The old rolltop desk," she murmured.

Then she held up the Woodstock T-shirt and the ticket stub. "Hmm," she said. "I see this in a frame. A sort of collage . . ."

She gave Anna and me a mischievous look. "Art. I see this as art. What do you girls think?"

We burst out laughing. Shaky, good laughter.

I thought Dad would be pleased.

CHAPTER 15

"Hey, is this meeting coming to order or what?" I asked, cramming a handful of potato chips in my mouth. Since the cupcake weekend, I'd sworn off sweets, at least for a while. But not junk food.

Kristy, who was lowering herself into the director's chair in Claudia's room, gave me an outraged look.

"What's the matter, Kristy? Getting a little behind in the job?" I asked. I pointed to the seat of the chair, which had just connected with the seat of her jeans, and burst out laughing at my own humor.

Kristy's mouth dropped open. Then Mary Anne snorted and a spray of potato chips flew out of her mouth.

That did it. Everyone started laughing. We were still laughing a few moments later when Mal rushed in saying, "I'm sorry I'm late, I — "

"It's okay," said Jessi. "We all get a little behind."

That set us off again, until the phone rang.

Instantly Kristy was all business. We stifled our laughter and Jessi leaned over to whisper something to Mal.

But Kristy had no sooner taken down the information and hung up, then Mal said to me, "That's a terrible joke. I'll have to tell the triplets."

We assigned the job and then Mal said, "Guess what. The carnival raised enough money to fund the arts programs in the Stoneybrook public schools for an entire year."

Claudia jumped up and did a little dance on her bed. Jessi applauded. Kristy let out a whistle between her teeth.

"What will happen when the year is up and the money runs out?" demanded Stacey.

Claudia stopped bouncing. "I guess we will have to hold another carnival."

"Piece of cake," said Jessi, smiling at me.

I groaned. "Not till next year!"

Mal took a call and Mary Anne flipped open the book. "The Papadakises for next Saturday night. Hmmmm. Kristy, you or Abby?"

I unconsciously tensed. Did Kristy still think I didn't have what it took to be a baby-sitter? I found myself staring at her, trying to read her thoughts.

But Kristy didn't even hesitate. "Abby can handle it. I have something to do."

"Kristy has a date," Stacey whispered very loudly.

I didn't hear Kristy's quick retort or join in the round of gentle laughter that followed. I was busy feeling good. I was off probation with Kristy.

And feeling at home with my friends in the BSC.

Just as Kristy was about to end the meeting, the phone rang. She picked it up. A grin spread across her face.

"Dawn!" she cried.

Everyone passed the phone around to say hello and tell Dawn about the carnival. When Mary Anne was finished, she handed the phone to me.

I was so surprised that I just sat there.

"Say hello to Dawn," Mary Anne prompted me. "You know about each other. So you might as well talk."

I held the phone to my ear. "Hello?"

"Hello!" Dawn's voice was friendly. I liked the sound of it immediately. We talked for a minute and then I said, "I've got to go. But I want you to know that I'm glad I'm the one who got to join the BSC."

"It's great, isn't it?" said Dawn cheerfully. "Good luck!"

I handed the phone back to Mary Anne so she could say good-bye.

Somehow, I felt that talking to Dawn had made me an official member of the BSC. I might not have a best friend in Stoneybrook, I might be a fast-moving, wisecracking sort of inexplicable blur to the others, but however I might seem, however different I might be, I belonged.

Not bad. Not bad at all.

That night, Anna and I had a domestic attack and decided to make dinner. From a recipe, not from a can or a box, okay?

"Let's make something that will keep till Mom gets home," Anna said.

"And something that will make the house smell good," I added, thinking of the nice smell of cupcakes baking. And the faint smell of old cologne.

We looked through Mom's cookbooks until we found a recipe that didn't seem too hard — turkey loaf.

"With peas," I said happily. I read from the suggested menu in the old cookbook, " 'In a nest of mashed potatoes.' "

"Toffuti splits for dessert," said Anna.

Anna and I talked while we made dinner. I told her about the BSC and about Kristy's deciding I'd Passed the Test.

"She had a date on Saturday night, I think," I concluded.

Anna ducked her head. "I've met a guy in the orchestra that I kind of like," she said.

I looked at my sister. My eyes opened wide. "Really? Seriously?"

"Not seriously!" said Anna. "Just as friends. I like him, but I don't *like* like him."

"Hmmm," I murmured.

The phone rang as we were putting the turkey in the oven.

"I'm calling from the station in the city," Mom said. "I just wanted to let you know I'm on my way home. I'll be there in a couple of hours."

I lifted my arm and pushed back my sleeve. I checked the heavy old watch on my wrist. "We've made dinner," I told Mom. "Whenever you get here, you'll be right on time."

I hung up the phone, smiling.

Dear Reader,

After Dawn returned to California, I was very happy to be able to create a new member of the Baby-sitters Club. The last new member I created was Jessi, and that was back in book number fourteen! There were so many things to decide — the character's personality, where she came from, what her family was like. And I wanted a character who was different from the other girls in the Baby-sitters Club. Many readers had asked for a character who is a twin. Many others had asked for a character who is Jewish. So we took these and other things into consideration, and created Abby and Anna Stevenson, whom you have just read about in Abby's very first book, *Welcome to the BSC, Abby*. And all you Dawn fans, take heart. Abby may be the new BSC member, but Dawn will always be a part of the Baby-sitters Club.

Happy reading,

Ann M Martin

L. GODWIN

Ann M. Martin

About the Author

ANN MATTHEWS MARTIN was born on August 12, 1955. She grew up in Princeton, NJ, with her parents and her younger sister, Jane.

Although Ann used to be a teacher and then an editor of children's books, she's now a full-time writer. She gets the ideas for her books from many different places. Some are based on personal experiences. Others are based on childhood memories and feelings. Many are written about contemporary problems or events.

All of Ann's characters, even the members of the Baby-sitters Club, are made up. (So is Stoneybrook.) But many of her characters are based on real people. Sometimes Ann names her characters after people she knows, other times she chooses names she likes.

In addition to the Baby-sitters Club books, Ann Martin has written many other books for children. Her favorite is *Ten Kids, No Pets* because she loves big families and she loves animals. Her favorite Baby-sitters Club book is *Kristy's Big Day*. (By the way, Kristy is her favorite baby-sitter!)

Ann M. Martin now lives in New York. She has two cats, Mouse and Rosie (who's a boy, but that's a long story). Her hobbies are reading, sewing, and needlework — especially making clothes for children.

Notebook Pages

This Baby-sitters Club book belongs to _____ .

I am _____ years old and in the _____ grade.

The name of my school is _____ .

I got this BSC book from _____ .

I started reading it on _____ and

finished reading it on _____ .

The place where I read most of this book is _____ .

My favorite part was when _____ .

If I could change anything in the story, it might be the part when

_____ .

My favorite character in the Baby-sitters Club is _____ .

The BSC member I am most like is _____

because _____ .

If I could write a Baby-sitters Club book it would be about _____

_____

_____ .

#90 Welcome to the BSC, Abby

Abby and Anna are Kristy's new neighbors. My neighbors are

_____ . The neighbor who

has lived next to me the longest is _____ .

My favorite neighbor is _____ because

_____ .

If I could have anyone I know move in next to me, I would want

it to be _____ . If I could

have any celebrity move in next to me, I would want it to be

_____ .

If I could have any BSC member for a neighbor, it would be

_____ because _____ .

The other members of the Baby-sitters Club are just getting to

know Abby. The friend I have that is most like Abby is _____

_____ because _____

_____ .

Abby likes to tell jokes. My favorite joke is _____

_____ . The funniest person

I know is _____ .

Look for #91

CLAUDIA AND THE FIRST
THANKSGIVING

Did I worry all that night? I did.

Was I completely tied up in knots by the time I reached my Short Takes class the next day?

I was.

It didn't help that the whole school seemed to have heard about the Big Thanksgiving Fight. I tried to follow Stacey's advice, to lay low and give vague answers to anyone who asked.

Ms. Garcia was standing by her desk as we came into the room. Needless to say, none of us was late. We all sat down without saying a word and faced Ms. Garcia. She looked gravely back at us.

When the bell rang, signaling the beginning of class, she said, "I'm afraid I have some bad news."

No one groaned or gasped. Somehow, no one was surprised.

"They killed our play, didn't they?" asked Rick.

"Not exactly," said Ms. Garcia. "But we have been given an ultimatum by the principal of Stoneybrook Elementary School, at the behest of the majority of her third grade teachers, and quite a few of her third-graders' parents. Either put on a play that shows the traditional first Thanksgiving story, or the principal will, er, kill the play."

Abby said, "That's censorship!"

Erica said, "Can they do that?"

"I believe it is censorship, too, Abby. And yes, Erica, they can do that," Ms. Garcia answered.

"What about our freedom of speech?" someone else said. "Or is that some made-up part of our history, too, just like Thanksgiving?"

"Wait a minute," I objected. "Thanksgiving is not made up. It's just been polished, and all the parts that people don't want to know about have been left out most of the time."

Fourteen pairs of eyes looked questioningly at me — including Stacey's.

THE BABY-SITTERS CLUB®

by Ann M. Martin

❑ MG43388-1	#1	Kristy's Great Idea	$3.50
❑ MG43387-3	#10	Logan Likes Mary Anne!	$3.50
❑ MG43717-8	#15	Little Miss Stoneybrook and Dawn	$3.50
❑ MG43722-4	#20	Kristy and the Walking Disaster	$3.50
❑ MG43347-4	#25	Mary Anne and the Search for Tigger	$3.50
❑ MG42498-X	#30	Mary Anne and the Great Romance	$3.50
❑ MG42508-0	#35	Stacey and the Mystery of Stoneybrook	$3.50
❑ MG44082-9	#40	Claudia and the Middle School Mystery	$3.25
❑ MG43574-4	#45	Kristy and the Baby Parade	$3.50
❑ MG44969-9	#50	Dawn's Big Date	$3.50
❑ MG44968-0	#51	Stacey's Ex-Best Friend	$3.50
❑ MG44966-4	#52	Mary Anne + 2 Many Babies	$3.50
❑ MG44967-2	#53	Kristy for President	$3.25
❑ MG44965-6	#54	Mallory and the Dream Horse	$3.25
❑ MG44964-8	#55	Jessi's Gold Medal	$3.25
❑ MG45657-1	#56	Keep Out, Claudia!	$3.50
❑ MG45658-X	#57	Dawn Saves the Planet	$3.50
❑ MG45659-8	#58	Stacey's Choice	$3.50
❑ MG45660-1	#59	Mallory Hates Boys (and Gym)	$3.50
❑ MG45662-8	#60	Mary Anne's Makeover	$3.50
❑ MG45663-6	#61	Jessi's and the Awful Secret	$3.50
❑ MG45664-4	#62	Kristy and the Worst Kid Ever	$3.50
❑ MG45665-2	#63	Claudia's Friend	$3.50
❑ MG45666-0	#64	Dawn's Family Feud	$3.50
❑ MG45667-9	#65	Stacey's Big Crush	$3.50
❑ MG47004-3	#66	Maid Mary Anne	$3.50
❑ MG47005-1	#67	Dawn's Big Move	$3.50
❑ MG47006-X	#68	Jessi and the Bad Baby-Sitter	$3.50
❑ MG47007-8	#69	Get Well Soon, Mallory!	$3.50
❑ MG47008-6	#70	Stacey and the Cheerleaders	$3.50
❑ MG47009-4	#71	Claudia and the Perfect Boy	$3.50
❑ MG47010-8	#72	Dawn and the We Love Kids Club	$3.50

More titles... ▶

The Baby-sitters Club titles continued...

❏ MG47011-6	#73 Mary Anne and Miss Priss	$3.50
❏ MG47012-4	#74 Kristy and the Copycat	$3.50
❏ MG47013-2	#75 Jessi's Horrible Prank	$3.50
❏ MG47014-0	#76 Stacey's Lie	$3.50
❏ MG48221-1	#77 Dawn and Whitney, Friends Forever	$3.50
❏ MG48222-X	#78 Claudia and Crazy Peaches	$3.50
❏ MG48223-8	#79 Mary Anne Breaks the Rules	$3.50
❏ MG48224-6	#80 Mallory Pike, #1 Fan	$3.50
❏ MG48225-4	#81 Kristy and Mr. Mom	$3.50
❏ MG48226-2	#82 Jessi and the Troublemaker	$3.50
❏ MG48235-1	#83 Stacey vs. the BSC	$3.50
❏ MG48228-9	#84 Dawn and the School Spirit War	$3.50
❏ MG48236-X	#85 Claudi Kishi, Live from WSTO	$3.50
❏ MG48227-0	#86 Mary Anne and Camp BSC	$3.50
❏ MG48237-8	#87 Stacey and the Bad Girls	$3.50
❏ MG22872-2	#88 Farewell, Dawn	$3.50
❏ MG22873-0	#89 Kristy and the Dirty Diapers	$3.50
❏ MG45575-3	Logan's Story Special Edition Readers' Request	$3.25
❏ MG47118-X	Logan Bruno, Boy Baby-sitter Special Edition Readers' Request	$3.50
❏ MG47756-0	Shannon's Story Special Edition	$3.50
❏ MG44240-6	Baby-sitters on Board! Super Special #1	$3.95
❏ MG44239-2	Baby-sitters' Summer Vacation Super Special #2	$3.95
❏ MG43973-1	Baby-sitters' Winter Vacation Super Special #3	$3.95
❏ MG42493-9	Baby-sitters' Island Adventure Super Special #4	$3.95
❏ MG43575-2	California Girls! Super Special #5	$3.95
❏ MG43576-0	New York, New York! Super Special #6	$3.95
❏ MG44963-X	Snowbound Super Special #7	$3.95
❏ MG44962-X	Baby-sitters at Shadow Lake Super Special #8	$3.95
❏ MG45661-X	Starring the Baby-sitters Club Super Special #9	$3.95
❏ MG45674-1	Sea City, Here We Come! Super Special #10	$3.95
❏ MG47015-9	The Baby-sitter's Remember Super Special #11	$3.95
❏ MG48308-0	Here Come the Bridesmaids Super Special #12	$3.95

Available wherever you buy books...or use this order form.

Scholastic Inc., P.O. Box 7502, 2931 E. McCarty Street, Jefferson City, MO 65102

Please send me the books I have checked above. I am enclosing $ _____ (please add $2.00 to cover shipping and handling). Send check or money order—no cash or C.O.D.s please.

Name _____ Birthdate _____

Address _____

City _____ State/Zip _____

Please allow four to six weeks for delivery. Offer good in the U.S. only. Sorry, mail orders are not available to residents of Canada. Prices subject to change.

BSC395

THE BABY-SITTERS CLUB®

ALL NEW!

by Ann M. Martin

Meet the best friends you'll ever have!

Have you heard? The BSC has a new look—and more great stuff than ever before. An all-new scrapbook for each book's narrator! A letter from Ann M. Martin! Fill-in pages to personalize your copy! Order today!

Now THE BABY-SITTERS CLUB®

★ is a Video Club too! ★

JOIN TODAY—

- Save $5.00 on your first video!
- 10-day FREE examination-before-you-keep policy!
- New video adventure every other month!
- Never an obligation to buy anything!

Now you can play back the adventures of America's favorite girls whenever you like. Share them with your friends too.

Just pop a tape into a VCR and watch *Claudia and the Mystery of the Secret Passage* or view *Mary Anne and the Brunettes, The Baby-sitters and the Boy Sitters, Dawn Saves the Trees* or any of the girls' many exciting, fun-packed adventures.

Don't miss this chance to actually see and hear Kristy, Stacey, Mallory, Jessi and the others in this new video series. Full details below.

■ ■ ■ CUT OUT AND MAIL TODAY! ■ ■ ■

MAIL TO: Baby-sitters Video Club • P.O. Box 30628 • Tampa, FL 33630-0628

Please enroll me as a member of the Baby-sitters Video Club and send me the first video, *Mary Anne and the Brunettes* for only $9.95 plus $2.50 shipping and handling. I will then receive other video adventures—one approximately every other month—at the regular price of $14.95 plus $2.50 shipping/handling each for a 10-day FREE examination. There is never any obligation to buy anything.

NAME	PLEASE PRINT
ADDRESS	APT.
CITY	
STATE	ZIP
BIRTH DATE	
( ) AREA CODE	DAYTIME PHONE NUMBER

CHECK ONE:

☐ I enclose $9.95 plus $2.50 shipping/handling.
☐ Charge to my card: ☐ VISA ☐ MASTERCARD ☐ AMEX

Card number_____ Expiration Date_____

Parent's signature:_____ 9AP S6